# SHAARA THE PRIESTESS

*(Book 7 In the Shaarvan Series)*

*Note: To start at the beginning of this series, please go to*
**Scholar-Ship-Bound**

## K.S. Riggin

# Table of Contents

# Main Characters & Places in the Shaarvan Series

**Altar:** Home of the Shapechanger & others (Altar is both the name of the planet and the capital city.)

**Altarians:** Those from the planet Altar.

**Baltoff:** The Old One on Westla who was manufacturing the drugs that Thenos used to overthrow the government of Altar.

**Barquel:** The main god worshipped on Freinana.

**Blair:** Owner of the Landoor ranch. Good guy.

**Brala:** Shaara's friend on Westla.

**Chaslow:** Shapechanger working for Thenos, blew up a nursery on Westla & hunted for Shaara.

**Clofa:** one of Altar's two moons. It was where the old Shapechanger liked to retire. Thenos blew it up.

**Crimson Black:** The horse-like landoor Shaara befriends.

**Flar:** Freinana, housemaster that Shaara stays with. Husband of Frieda.

**Frieda:** Freinana housemistress that Shaara stays with. Wife of Flar.

**Goria:** Pseudo wife of Pathe. Former lover of Shaarvan. Bad person.

**Isandor:** The Commoner who owns Shaara on Freinana. Bad guy.

**Landoor:** An animal that looks similar to a horse.

**Pathe:** Son of Tevor & Teea (brother of Shaarvan & Thenos.) Doctor, good guy.

**Saberey:** Symbol of the Shapechanger & their origin.

**Shaandar: (Thandar)** son of Thalia and Thal, adopted by Shaarvan. Also called Prince Thenon by the Commoners since Thenos declared him his son.

**Shaara:** College student. Wife of Shaarvan and later Stegthal (Thal.) Renamed numerous times: Susan, Sletttha, Sleena, Skeva, Thalia, Thenosa.

**Shaarac: (Thaarac, Thenon)** Shaara and Shaarvan's son.

**Shaarvan:** Steals his wife, Shaara, from a college campus, Altarian Shapechanger.

**Skeva:** Name given to Shaara on Freinana.

**Sleena:** Name given to Shaara on Freinana.

**Slettha:** Slaver's name for Shaara on Freinana.

**Spelon:** One of Shaara's guardians. Shapechanger Warrior becomes Shaara's lover later.

**Starnkor:** Teea's Second Husband.

**Stegthal: (Thal)** He becomes Shaara's Second Husband. Good & bad.

**Susan:** Shaara's original Earth name.

**Targone**: Shapechanger who arrives on Freinana to verify that Shaara is Shapechanger.

**Teea:** Shaarvan's mother, lives on Altar, wife of Tevor (and later Starnkor.)

**Tem:** Head of Westla, Uncle to Shaarvan, Tevor's brother.

**Temina:** Wife of Tem, mentally unstable.

**Tenor:** One of Shaara's guardians. Shapechanger Warrior.

**Tessa:** High Priestess.

**Tevor:** Shaarvan's father lives on Altar, and husband of Teea.

**Thal:** Stegthal's name on Deathstar.

**Thalia:** Shaara's name on Deathstar.

**Thaandar: (Thenon) (Shaandar)** Shaara & Thal's son. Shaarvan adopts him.

**Thedar:** One of Shaara's guardians. Shapechanger Warrior.

**Theinian:** A group of assorted members, usually slavers and most often gay.

**Thenos:** Son of Tevor & Teea (brother of Shaarvan & Pathe), Bad guy.

**Thenosa:** Thenos' name for Shaara.

**Tren:** Owner of the casino and of Shaara. Good guy to Shaara.

**Tura:** The Priestess medic who rode the ship with them to Altar.

**Westla:** Huge artificial satellite. Only Shapechanger may go there, or girls and servants.

## Additional Terminology:

**Tide:** Approximately one Earth Tide. Tides are usually grouped, as in a fiveTide, twentyTide, etc.

**Pass:** Approximately one year. A halfPass and a quarterPass are common expressions.

**Shapechanger**: Never found in the plural. The Shapechanger is an artificially derived species that is capable of changing their shape, most often as a Saberey (tiger-like cat). This ability also includes many sensory improvements and abilities.

**The Names of Shapechanger:** Names beginning with T or S denote Power. Those Shapechanger are deemed Lords. Formal testing on Westla ranks them.

**Warrior Shapechanger:** Those who meet qualifications of specific battle readiness. The ranking is by formal tests on Westla.

**Priestess:** Females who have achieved a ranking on Westla denoting their ability to stand up against Shapechanger Power. They are also given respect and special treatment.

# *Chapter One*

## Tren

We had left them all behind on the ship: my sweet, sad-eyed Shaara, her guardians, who were now my friends, and the two little children I had grown to love. I had not been Shapechanger long enough to fully know Shapechanger's ways, but I knew Shaarvan well enough to know his Power. When he demanded, whether his eyes flared green with Shapechanger Power or not, most of us had no choice but to obey. He said to come with him to Altar, and I nodded, said my goodbye to all, and headed with him to his ship, bound for Altar.

He was now my older brother, the temporary head of the Trendacons on Altar for as long as his father remained in a coma, and unless I misunderstood, also the general of the Shapechanger army. He was a big shot in his world. But my heart remained on Shaara's ship. I did not want to leave her. She was the whole reason I had gotten into this mess.

She was once my slave — a dirt-smeared little girl dressed in the rags of a male street ruffian. I had won her in a poker game. But when I went to claim my prize, I suspected her of being Shapechanger. Those lovely gray eyes of hers, the way she sent tentacles into my mind, urging me to do things, I more than suspected. I was sure. So I did not do what my body urged me when I saw her naked. Instead, I notified the Shapechanger Guild, then regretted it every day after that because, in the small amount of time of my ownership, I had fallen in love.

From the moment that mischievous imp came into my life, everything shifted. I had even agreed to make her my wife, although a gambling casino owner like me had absolutely no business with a wife, especially one who loved riding landoors and stank like a field hand most of the time.

But then her husband, a wealthy Altarian, had come for his kidnapped wife and, instead of rewarding me for notifying them, had claimed me for the Shapechanger. Being forced into transition against my will had further uprooted my life. But the carrot had been that I could see Shaara again. And I had lived with her, her bondmates, and the children for a while. But now, I was once again being torn away by the husband who no longer wanted her.

The Fates play mean tricks on us. I was most resentful.

I sulked for a twoTide, then I remembered my promise to Shaara and began to badger Shaarvan.

Tide after Tide, I reminded Shaarvan of what he had left behind, a wife as taste-worthy as *Brilla Brandy* (the alcohol, not some female I had never met) with eyes that melted you, lips like rose petals fresh with the dew of morning, and the most tantalizing of all smiles, along with the sweetest, saucy nature that made you want to roll over and beg for her attention. I said it all, hoping to catch his interest, but Shaarvan remained granite-hard in his resolve not to return for her.

"Tell me about how you got your casino," Shaarvan began one morning.

"Not a fitting place for Shaara, I fear. I was debating selling it. As you know, Shaara is too gentle for such places. What do you think? Could Shaara adapt to the ragtag element you saw in the place?"

Shaarvan sipped his beverage and stared out into the darkness visible through the ship's passing. He sighed, then changed the conversation. "You will enjoy Altar. You can choose a new existence there, another casino, if you like, a higher class one, if that would make you feel better. You will be honored and respected on Altar since you are now a Trendacons."

He was trying hard, persuasive as a fish peddler telling you his old fish was fresh. But no deal. I wouldn't take his stinky fish or the topic avoidance.

"What did Shaara like to do on Altar? What was her favorite activity? How did she spend her time?"

He might have turned slightly green. I knew it couldn't be air sickness. He was a ship's pilot. His face twisted as if his stomach hurt. He put down his cup and sighed.

"You will like my mother. She is very emotional still. She will welcome you with open arms. You will be her new son, you know."

"Yes, Shaara told me about her. Your wife said that she and Teea have a good relationship. She said some of her happiest memories were spending time with Teea and your father. Something about a game she was learning to play?"

I was incessant. Shaarvan's sighs grew thicker. His easy flow tapered off, and he began to look beaten by my assaults. Shaara's bondmates, my friends, had told me that Shaarvan was a good guy. They had once been his friends, and I supposed they still were, although none of them approved of Shaarvan deserting his wife and ordering her to go to Westla for Priestess training.

If he really was the leader of the Shapechanger forces and had been in battle for more than a Pass, then he should be used to a barrage of missiles shooting his way. I was a general, too, because he had crushed my girl, sent her into tears and a depression so deep that even her beloved landoor, Crimson Black, might not be able to pull her out of it.

So I kept up my harassment as the ship flew further away on its return to Altar.

One day I told Shaarvan about the swim Shaara and I had taken together when I believed us to be bonded. "I had finally decided to make her mine," I said.

Shaarvan did not react. His face remained blank, devoid of emotion. I wanted to kick him into action.

"I ordered Shaara to take off her clothes and swim with me. I would have seduced her in that lake if Targone hadn't come by and pried us apart."

Shaarvan's eyes flared green then. But it lasted no more than a minute. He was standing, leaning against the wall of the control room, his foot resting on a chair. He shifted and set his foot down. I think he was about to retreat once more from my steady needling.

"I was going to marry her, you know," I said, grinding in the point. "I would have, too, if you had not alerted us to your presence. And then, when you finally arrived, and I saw you with her, I thought that she really meant something to you, that you loved her. That was the only reason I backed away, giving you the room to woo her back."

I think he let out a growl. But it was a low-voiced, non-aggressive tone. Yet, the challenge issued in that sound worried me that I might have gone too far, but Shaarvan remained immovable. His stubbornness must have planted him in a road mixture thick enough to anchor him to a stupidity post.

After he left me alone once more, I pondered what bullets I had left to shoot at him. But if swimming nude with his wife and painting guilt trips hadn't budged his buttocks into some kind of realization that he was acting like an absolute idiot, what was left?

But there was more to say, and so I kept on saying it. I talked about our adventures on the moon of that strange planet and, later, onboard the ship. I told him how Shaara had never stopped mourning his absence and had received most of her punishments due to arguing about how he would one day come back for her.

"Spelon jabbed at her continuously, arguing that you didn't want her, that she was Thal's. I guess he was right."

Shaarvan's sandwich went uneaten. He left me to finish my meal on my own. I would have chuckled if I had believed I had actually scored a point, but Shaarvan was a tough one. I could not read him. Was he really punishing Shaara for attaining Priestess, for disobeying his order? Was that was his obstinacy was about?

There was more, but he accepted all my words without question or comment. At those moments, he was not a Saberey tiger but a granite rock, a permanent mountain of unfeeling coldness. Forgive me, Shaara. I wanted to tell her across the stars, but that was only something Shaarvan could do. I was not her Saberey mate. I truly wished . . .

"We all adore Shaara, you know. We practically worship the ground she walks on. We hate seeing what you are doing to her."

No response but to sip at his drink. His eyes remained shuttered, as they had been throughout our journey.

"When Thal beat her, it was I who interceded. The others were too fixated in Shapechanger law to interfere between a husband and wife. But I love her, you see," I said brazenly to the Shapechanger who officially owned her.

9

Did Shaarvan punch me for my disrespect? No. Did he hang his head a moment in regret for turning her over to Thal? No. If I were notching winning nicks, he was the cold, uninterested observer.

"You must feel some remorse for not being there to save her from Thal's brutality," I poked at him.

He got up from the table, filled up his cup with more hot brew and said, "If you will excuse me. I have some reading to do, my brother."

"Thal almost killed her, but you are the cause of her greatest pain. You, when you turned your back and left her again."

He continued on as if he hadn't heard me, walking to another place on the ship, somewhere away from me.

But I didn't stop my torment. And then, finally, as Altar came into view, I said the words that had been on the tip of my tongue throughout our voyage together.

"It is obvious that you do not want her, Shaarvan. Give Shaara to me. Let me see if I can put the sunshine back in her eyes."

Shaarvan turned to me with the first sign of anger he had displayed the whole trip.

"Never," he said. "She is free now. I will never again give Shaara to anyone."

# Shaarvan

I needed a brother, one who could make me forget what I was leaving behind, but instead, I got a nagging guilt-maniac who tortured me the entire flight.

Did he think I did not know the true nature of Shaara? She was my backbone, an arm and a leg. She was not only a part of me but my best part. Did he forget how I had searched for her most of a Pass, dreading to find her crippled in slavery? I had dreamed of her each night, haunted by the weakness inside me that had allowed her to be stolen from me.

And all through the war, I battled between what I wanted, which was Shaara, and what was best for her. Yes, there was Shaarac, as well. I should have been thinking of my young son, but every dream I had was of Shaara. I breathed her breath when none could travel that far. I smelled her fragrance and heard her voice. She was my every thought — the one I must protect at all costs.

I had told her once that I would die for her, and I had because I'd given her to another, knowing that was the death of my soul. My poor Shaara. It has been torture for both of us, this unending misery.

But Tren, my new brother, does not see that. He does not understand the wounds that fester inside me because I left her again. She is with her guardians. They all love her. Spelon has gentled from the Warrior I used to know, the one so full of pride he couldn't feel the void in his soul. I know he is obsessed with her. She will be fine.

She will go to Priestess training and be happier than she ever was with my demands and constant criticisms of her daring spirit. I see that now. She was always too strong with Power to bow down to me. No wonder I called her *difficult* all the time.

I must let her go to find the freedom she struggled so hard to attain. I know it is best for her, and I must be okay with that.

Perhaps one Tide my sons will come to live with me. Tessa told me that Shaara would be the Institute's High Priestess heir. The soothsayer recognized the greatness of the young Terran girl even then. High Priestess, head of the Westla Institute, surely that will appease any loss that Shaara feels for my leaving her.

We are almost home. Altar stares at us through our panel. Perhaps the war has ended while I was gone. If not, I am healthy again. I will be stronger now, better able to lead them to victory.

My mother will no doubt also criticize me for leaving her daughter behind. She will not understand my decision. But I have brought her a new son. Tren must be enough for her. It is all I can offer, for Shaara deserves her autonomy. She has become a Priestess.

# Shaara

It has been a long trip back to Westla, not in the passage of time, but in grief. Spelon worked me hard in the gym. I jogged the ship, practiced my Power, read books, practiced languages, and played with my children. In the nights, Spelon comforted me. Through the days, I felt the love of my bondmates.

I was never bored. I was never alone. But whenever I closed my eyes. I could still see Shaarvan, turning his back and walking away. Again.

I missed Tren, too. I once loved him. I still do, just not in the same way. I am glad he is my brother now. I know he will keep his promise and talk to Shaarvan, but my husband should not need words to force him back to me. If he didn't feel love inside him, then all was lost.

My guardians surrounded me. We were family, as Tenor kept saying. I did my best not to wear my sadness around them. I pushed smiles on my face. I forced myself to eat. I showed them my affection whenever I thought about it.

Thedar talked about my training with Tessa. He told me stories from his home world, Nardan. I was eager to listen. Sometimes, he enfolded me in his arms and whispered, "The war will end, and then he will want you back, little Shaara. Do not suffer so much."

Is suffering quantitative? How much is so much, too much, not enough?

But I did not speak such thoughts. I hugged him back, then left to give Thaandar another bottle, to play a game with Shaarac, or to go sob in my room. Again.

Another Tide saw Tenor playing the same game. His words were kind. His promises were as well-meaning as Thedar's. I hugged him, too, and thanked him for cheering me up.

I knew how lucky I was to have these wonderful Shapechanger in my life. I was rich, but my heart didn't feel that way. My heart hurt.

~~~~~~

The ship's warning bells sounded. We didn't need them. We could see Westla through the panel. The great Saberey eye was staring at us. Our ship did all the official stuff, identifying us and receiving back our okays for landing. Thal's ship was a modern wonder and well-known by West's Space Port. No red flags raised to stop our entrance into the Space Port.

The Great Saberey Eye opened, and we descended. Shaarac was old enough to be excited. He chattered the whole way down. I used to be full of amazement at such things. Once I was even fearful, but then I had Shaarvan at my side to reassure me. I guess I am now an experienced spacer, used to rejection and feeling like discarded waste.

The ship settled down into its reserved spot. Thal had long ago bought the berth, so no other ship could take his spot. That meant that the drama of our placement at Westla's Space Port was nil. Or it would have been if Thal had not left his shipboard room to join us.

Thal was normally kept far away from me. He hadn't been locked in his quarters, but the guardians had warned him they would do so if he came near me. Such precautions had been initiated after he had beaten me up, almost sending me to my death.

The moment Thal entered the control room, my guardians surrounded the children and me, making sure to keep my ex-husband separated from us.

Thal owned the ship we were on, so it was difficult to forbid him from being present at our set down on Westla, but his madness came on in unpredictable fits. Sometimes, he was recognizable as the Shapechanger of old. Other times, he was a stranger to me, one who lived in the fantasy of still owning me.

I was holding Thaandar, his son. I worried, as did my Shapechanger Warrior guardians, that Thal might demand to hold the baby or me, but Thal didn't. His focus was solely on our landing. He was already issuing orders to Tenor about which books should be carted first to his residence. Tenor ignored him, except for a couple of nods at the appropriate times.

Spelon had been holding Shaarac, my other son, but with Thal's arrival, Spelon shifted the boy to Thedar. I expected that Spelon wanted his hands free in case he needed to protect us from a possible bout of Thal's insane anger. But, although Spelon was prepared, Thal was too busy overseeing what obviously didn't need his micro-management.

"Why don't you stay here and organize your materials," Tenor suggested to Thal when my former husband started talking about departing from the ship.

Thal shot him a glance, then noticed me. "Good suggestion, Tenor. Spelon, take Thalia to our quarters on Westla. Make sure she obeys. No tantrums," he ordered, glaring at me.

I lowered my eyes. I didn't need to anymore, but it seemed easier than reminding Thal that he was no longer in charge of me. Besides, it was better for my older son if everything remained calm.

Shaarac, in Thedar's arms, looked unsure about the situation. Shaarvan had explained how he was the child's real father and that Thal was unwell and could no longer fulfill that position. But then Shaarvan had headed back to the Altar, Thal was back again, acting like he was in charge. It must be very confusing for Shaarac.

Even worse, Shaarvan, in his distress over the Priestess thing, hadn't even said good-bye to his young son, and now Thal, after his long absence from Shaarac, completely ignored the boy's presence. Would Shaarac think both of his fathers had deserted him?

Thedar was holding Shaarac and speaking softly to him. The boys always had my Shapechanger bondmates to love and care for them. At least there was that.

I felt moisture threatening at the back of my eyes from the guilt I felt concerning both Shapechanger, but I resisted the tears. The path forward might be twisted, but it was still a good path. I would get training with the Priestess Guild at the Institute, as Shaarvan had ordered, and then I would take the boys to Altar. Everything would be fine then. I had to believe that.

Yet each time I closed my eyes, I kept picturing Shaarvan as he turned away from me, rejecting me as his wife. He'd been angry.

Maybe he'd already changed his mind and remembered that he loved me.

Tren had gone on the ship with Shaarvan. My friend (and new brother) had promised he would talk to Shaarvan and persuade him that the two of us needed each other.

But I had disobeyed Shaarvan's orders. I had become a Priestess in order to kill his brother. Big flaws in a Shapechanger wife and the penalty for such rebellion would be steep. I had known that even before I made the decision. Yet sometimes, when something needs to be done, you have to do it yourself, no matter the consequences.

Thenos had been evil. He'd killed thousands of innocents. He'd started a war on Altar, proclaiming himself emperor. He'd planned to kill Shaarvan, my older son, and all the other people I loved. I figured that was just cause for my sacrifice.

But right now, we were back on Westla, and I was sinking into bad memories. It was time to move forward.

Thal retreated back to his quarters, where he kept his research, telescopes, books, and analysis. Sorting through that would keep him busy for a while. He might even forget to start packing. Separation was a good thing for the boys and for me.

The rest of us had no need to take anything with us. Westla would provide all that we required. I surveyed the main room of the ship one last time, picturing the time we'd sat at the table playing a card game, which I had repeatedly won unless my bondmates cheated to allow me that. I'd never been sure. The table was where Shaarvan had sat, finally, after all these Passes, listening to something I had to say. Tren had been the cause of that. He'd spoken in favor of my speaking, and the others had supported me.

Goodbye, ship, I wanted to say, but that was silly. I must leave such fanciful thoughts behind me. I was a mother of two children with full rights. And I was a Priestess.

Spelon placed his arm around my shoulder. "Are you ready?" he asked.

Life was about *change*. I'd heard that said as if change was a good thing. Who had told me that? Was it Shaarvan's mother or his father? Whoever had proclaimed it to be true, I agreed with them. Living was moving forward and changing.

I smiled at Spelon, something new in our relationship. Then, checking that Tenor had the baby and Thedar had Shaarac's hand, I set forward, stepping through the open portal and onto the ramp of Westla's Space Port.

Westla was a place that I'd never wanted to go, the artificial world that Shaarvan had brought me to Passes ago. But there were good memories on Westla. My guardians had taken me to see the mountains for skiing. We'd gone to the zoo, the arboretum, the forests, and a museum. Tessa lived on Westla, and so did Tem, my uncle.

My footsteps were muted. I wore firm-based shoes, comfortable shoes, but my tread was not as heavy as that of the three Shapechanger males. My bondmates were Warriors, muscle-heavy all over. They were agile and skilled in battle-readiness. They knew moves that would disable anyone who attacked, even without the pipe weapons hanging across their backs. But their footfall was a flat echo, the dull thumps of an army on military march. How strange when there were only three of them now.

I missed Tren, my owner from Freinana, who'd become Shaarvan's brother and now mine. Sometimes I even missed Thal until I recalled the way he'd beaten me and ripped my soul binding away. He'd turned into an Isandor, another male I'd sent into the depths of insanity.

"She's feeling guilt for Thal, Spelon," Tenor said.

Sometimes, I projected my emotions, but I'd been better at not doing so. "How did you...?"

"Your scent, Shaara," Spelon smirked. His amusement flooded the air with the odd mixture of gardenia and cherry blossoms. I'd entertained him, apparently.

"You have nothing to feel guilt over, little one," Tenor said. "Thal caused his own punishment. It was not your fault, Shaara."

Spelon's flowery odor made wave for grape bubblegum. He wasn't good at hiding his emotions either.

Tenor laughed. "You are loved," he reminded me. "We all feel that way, but only Spelon farts his feelings."

I giggled, probably inappropriately, but I think Tenor wanted me to do so. We'd all had a lot of heaviness to tread through in the halfPass since Shaarvan left. Guilt, irritation, and anger were odors we'd become familiar with.

Thaandar, in Tenor's arms, was wide-eyed at the ships all around us. His usual goo and gah baby talk had quieted as if allowing him to concentrate on his surroundings. Although he normally would be asking for me to carry him, "mmm," with arms flailing, he seemed content to be held by Tenor.

My other son, Shaarac was the one I worried over. Had he been hurt by Thal's obliviousness to his presence?

"Shaarac is fine," Spelon said, attuned to my thoughts.

We glanced over to Thedar and Shaarac. Thedar was talking to him, telling him about the different ships. My son looked like he wasn't spending any time worrying over his father's rejection — both fathers, since a Shapechanger husband viewed the arrival of a child from a Second Husband as his own.

Our steps had taken us beyond the ship's berthing area to the concourse of Westla arrivals. We'd soon be passing through the decontamination areas. I remembered what had happened the last time. The chemicals in the spray had awakened a need inside me so great that I'd practically climbed up Shaarvan in my urge to join.

Should I warn the others? Spelon would be happy to service me, but it would be very embarrassing.

I was sure that the containment would hold only Spelon and me. Tenor and Thedar would each take one of the boys through. Thankfully, they wouldn't see my reaction.

"Spelon, I need to tell you something," I said as I steered him away from Tenor.

"This is an unwise separation, Shaara," Spelon warned.

"I . . .I reacted badly last time in the decontamination chamber."

"Oh, yes. Not uncommon. We shall enjoy it, my spitball."

"I don't want . . ."

"No more separation from the others, Shaara. You need to be guarded. Others do not know that you are dangerous. They might attack."

I nodded and allowed Spelon to lead us back to Tenor. Thedar had stopped, too. He waited for us to come closer.

"Problem?" he asked.

"Only the good kind," Spelon said with a smirk.

There were times that Spelon was a good guy, kind and considerate. But sometimes, I wanted to throw a shoe at him. This was one of them.

# *Chapter Two*

## Spelon

It was disappointing that the spray brought on no wild abandonment of Shaara's sexual inhibitions. Perhaps the high-level Shaara had attained discarded such chemical interference. It would have been good for her. A little fun added pleasure to life. Shaara has forgotten how to savor small moments of joy, and she carries immense loads on her delicate shoulders. None of us can get her to shake them off.

As much as I disliked the High Priestess Tessa, I think her training will be good for Shaara. Perhaps Tessa can help Shaara to release her guilt. First killing can be overwhelming even for a male Warrior, and then to disobey her conditioning with Shaarvan and to be rejected by him . . . Yes, there was much for Shaara to put aside.

I have the feeling from what Tren said, that Tessa knew exactly what Shaara would do, what she needed to do. Tessa's visions were far-seeing. Not even Tem discounted them. Hopefully, Tessa would know how to help our girl bring back her smiles.

The boys will be fine. I know Shaara worries about them, but they are Shapechanger. They accept change more readily than females do.

# Tenor

We had already discussed the protocol for our arrival. Shaara had not been part of that conversation since she'd been playing with her sons. We felt she needed that time with them, although I am sure she would have resented our making decisions without her. She has gotten prickly about that, so intent on reminding us of her new position she only rarely slips back into the Shaara we knew. But then, she is still grieving Shaarvan's rejection.

Of course, we realized that she no longer needed to bow to our governance. That was a difficult change for us, as well, but not one of us doubted that she had earned those rights. (Not that it would make a difference how we felt about it, except to rob us of her friendship.) We were all learning new paths.

Unfortunately, she was still a child in her knowledge of the Shapechanger world. She did not seem to have the ability yet to discern danger from acceptable risk. Perhaps we can get some guidance from Tessa, but I doubt her receptivity. The High Priestess did not offer much assistance before.

No. Tem will likelier be the one with answers. I was sure he would have expertise in cautioning appropriately without conveying demands. Maybe Shaara would listen to him because he was the head of her family and of Westla — and because he was Shaarvan's uncle.

There was also the matter of Thal. We must inform Tem of the circumstances of Thal's madness. Would the clinic be able to guide our former friend back to mental stability?

Shaarvan had informed us that we must report our arrival to Tem the moment we returned. We will do so, but in all honesty, the three of us would have preferred to return to our accommodations, assuming our former residences were still available. I supposed that was another reason for speaking to Tem immediately. He would be the one to provide us with adequate shelter and provision us with financial support, according to Shaarvan.

Since we would be attending and guarding Shaarvan's sons, our role continued. Did we dare leave out the part of Shaara's unwelcomeness in our little family? No, Tem must be told everything. He would probably dig deep into our minds anyway, at least enough to discover any left-out information. Surely, he would not agree with Shaarvan on the matter.

Besides, Shaara was a Priestess. She would not be cast out just because she disobeyed her husband.

Too many thoughts were swimming through my brain. It was good that the baby was asleep. My energy felt depleted. Shaara was not the only one dealing with an overabundance of stress.

# Shaara

I should have asked where we were going instead of relying on the males to decide. It would be so easy to slip back into the obedient *child* as Thedar used to call me. (Well, not the obedient part.)

I will not be obedient. I must learn to take responsibility except I don't know how. Returning to Westla was almost like being dropped in Freinana without any background. Where should we go? What was first on the list? And the boys, how could I take care of them if I were training with Tessa or enrolled in the Institute? I needed my bondmates. But I leaned on them too much. I needed to grow up.

Tessa would help me pull it all together, except I didn't even know how to get to her residence. The Shapechanger had always escorted me. How did Tessa get around without guards? How did she know what to do?

Thedar, perhaps feeling my concerns, moved closer. Spelon was preoccupied with guard duty, and Thedar was always attuned to my mental fidgets. Thedar said nothing, but his eyes held mine, and he nodded his head. Shaarac waved to me, his smile big and full of dimples. Between the two of them, I couldn't help the smile that crept back on my face.

We had not yet entered the interior halls of Westla, yet Spelon resumed his Warrior pose, pipe on guard. Was Westla that dangerous? Should I be ready to give battle? But no, my bondmates would not allow that. They would push me behind them and treat me like Shaarac and the baby.

"I can smell your worry. Do you not trust that we will guide you safely?" Thedar asked.

"I trust you," I whispered. I wanted my independence, but I didn't want to hurt Thedar's feelings. Besides, I was as lost in the city of West as Shaarac would have been.

"We must go to Tem's court first. We shall check in with him to see if our residences are still available. It is possible they were given to someone else." Thedar told me.

Another worry. I had not even thought of that. I guess I assumed that we would stay where we had before. But that had been Passes ago. Someone might be living there. What if there were no empty residences? Would we have to return to the ship to sleep?

Thedar reached out and touched my arm. "We will be okay. We will do whatever it takes to assure you are taken care of. You know that."

Again, I nodded. Assurance was a flaky thing. Mine was shredding bits of detritus as we walked. Would I leave a trail, like dandruff cast off by a good brushing?

"What if Tem forbids me to stay with you and the boys?" I asked. "What should I do then?"

"Then we will give battle, Shaara." Despite Spelon's possible objections to his comforting me, since Spelon was often territorial, Thedar swung his left arm about my shoulder and pulled me toward him. I briefly leaned my head against his chest, but it was awkward. Thedar was holding Shaarac, who seemed to be nodding off, exhausted from all the excitement.

I was grateful that Thedar was dealing with that issue. Shaarac was big for his age and too weighty for me to be able to hold him long. I couldn't have carried my son a block without gasping for breath. Thedar, like my other guardians, was super strong.

"We shall never leave you without support, Child. You know that. You are ours . . ."

I started to argue with that statement. It was too much of a claiming, but Thedar stopped me with a fierce look.

"You are ours, and we are yours," he said, then smiled down at me with his perfect smile, the one that sent waves of love through my body.

I had three bondmates who all seemed to adore me and my two sons. Spelon had taken over the bed-sharing activities since female Shapechanger were needy in that area, but Thedar and Tenor still treated me like kind fathers — strict but well-meaning. I was grateful

25

for their patience with me and for their instructions, no matter how uncomfortable such words of wisdom often were.

We were approaching the final corner. I recalled how it led us into the grand entry. We'd be in the city of West at that point. Spelon must have heard something. He called out, "Weapons."

I took Shaarac from Thedar.

"Behind me," Thedar ordered, and without thought, I moved to obey.

# Spelon

It wasn't the first time I'd thought about the need for more guards for Shaara. She was too pleasing to be ignored by the unattached Shapechanger. Of course, attacking a Shapechanger wife would be a death sentence, but the young males rarely concerned themselves with what might befall them in the future. The chance to be with her carnally was everything. A passionate Power merge was an enticement not obtained by sex with a willing servant girl.

I checked the readiness of my mates and of Shaara. It was not good. Shaara was behind Thedar, who was ready. He was fully weaponed, but Tenor had his hands full with the baby. The boy was asleep, but a baby in hand would leave Tenor practically defenseless. It would be up to me to defend our group. I hoped I would be enough.

I debated a moment. Should I creep forward, destroying the surprise of their attack, or launch a wild and noisy sprint of aggression in the hopes of frightening them away? Neither was a suitable plan, but I chose the latter. It would at least send me forward, away from the children and Shaara. Perhaps my family could retreat back to one of the entrance chambers.

I charged forward, growling and bellowing with the full volume of my Saberey roar. But almost immediately, I slammed on the brakes. What I saw made my snarls die. No Shapechanger youths stood there waiting to capture our woman. It was Tem and a group of guards, plus Tessa.

"It's alright," I yelled back. "Come on forward. Our friends are here."

Thedar escorted Shaara. He'd taken back our older boy. Tenor was right behind them, almost touching. Their eyes widened in disbelief.

It was said that Tem almost never left his assembly hall, yet here he was, prepared to greet our arrival.

Tessa moved forward. Her arms widened as she scooped Shaara into her arms. The High Priestess of Westla wasn't a big woman, but most females were larger than Shaara. But what both lacked in size, they made up for in spirit.

"Welcome home," I heard Tessa say. "We are proud of you."

A young woman stepped forward. She was not a Shapechanger but a servant girl. She held her arms out to take Thaandar. Tenor looked at me to make the decision. I nodded, knowing that Tem trusted the servant or she would not be there.

"Shaarac?" Tem said, his eyes almost instantly noting the child in Thedar's arms. "May I?" he asked, but without waiting for a reply, he strode forward and took the boy.

Meanwhile, Shaara was even more tightly enveloped by Tessa's embrace. Her eyes looked to me for assistance.

"Let her breathe, Tessa," I said, daring greatly because Tessa had formerly not been kind to my bondmates and me.

But this time, Tessa took a step back and laughed.

"You have grown. All of you have grown except Shaarvan. He is slow."

"He is not here," I said before I realized that Tessa was not referring to whether he was with us or not. Priestesses were often difficult to follow. They spoke weirdly.

I threw my arm around Shaara's shoulders in case she needed support. Her eyes were glazed with tears, but I saw her resistance to them. She was becoming more Warrior every Tide.

"Come," Tem said. "There is seating over there. We can chat for a moment. There is much to tell, much to hear."

# Tenor

I had never been this close to the High One of Westla. Thal and Shaarvan had held meetings each Tide before Shaarvan's departure. But Thedar, Spelon, and I had stayed out of the politics of it. Our job had been to keep Shaara and Shaarac safe and entertained and to ease her opposition for what was to come. Mainly, we tried to cheer her up.

But in those delightful times, we had experienced Shaara's laughter, her sparkling eyes, and the way she had favored us with gentle smiles once she got over her fear of us — those were happy times.

But now, we were beside the great one and sitting next to Tessa, the Supreme Priestess, the scariest woman in West — no, on the whole planet of Westla.

At first, I said nothing. Not even when Tem's servant girl took the baby from my hold. But when we were sitting down, and Tem began asking us about the Pass we'd spent on uninhabited planets to avoid Thenos, I found myself adding details here and there: the stubras, which still lit up Shaara's eyes, the gardens we'd planted, the water channels that had irrigated it, and the way we had twice needed to flee in the middle of the night when Thenos invaded Shaara's dreams.

When we'd unraveled various details, then Tem asked about the big event. He somehow knew about Thenos' death. Had Tessa foreseen it? Had Tem received word from Shaarvan?

Tem responded to that query. Yes, they had heard from the Shapechanger. Shaarvan and Tren were back on Altar. The war was lessening, and the Commoners had lost their impetus to give challenge after the death of their King Emperor.

Tessa cackled then. "They still want Shaara, though. And the younger boy. They call her Thenosa, and he, Theron."

Shaara's eyes widened. The smell of almonds permeated the air. Spelon slipped his arm around her shoulder again, calming her fears. "We will never let them take you, Shaara. Never. You are safe, and the boys are safe."

The Priestess cackled again. "She is safe on Altar. They don't want to hurt her or the child. They want to crown her Queen and dub the baby Crown Prince."

# *Chapter Three*

## Shaara

The moment I stopped gasping, my first thought was how angry Shaarvan was going to be.

Tessa immediately crowed loud enough to break our eardrums. Then she screeched like a tortured cat. Spelon drew me closer, although he couldn't really protect me from Westla's High Priestess. She was a force, I think, even stronger than Tem. I watched her, in case retreat was necessary, but with less alarm than if I'd never spent time with her. Anyone who'd been around her long knew she made strange noises.

At last, she took in a deep breath, then shook her head. "You are still a fool, young Terran girl."

Thedar immediately spoke up in my defense. Unwisely, perhaps, but appreciated. "She is not a girl. As you know, the law states that a woman who has two children is fully Shapechanger with all its rights."

"Yes, and she's a Priestess," Spelon added. "So you're doubly wrong."

I swear the whole group gasped and swayed backward. Not because of the Priestess part. Tessa probably already knew about that, but because Spelon had said that Tessa was *wrong*.

I reached over and took Spelon's hand. If Tessa were going to attack him for his honesty, I'd make sure she knew that I'd be protecting him.

"You have won them over, then," Tessa said, fastening her beady eyes on me. "You have converted Shapechanger bullies to. . ."

"Enough, Tessa," Tem said in a voice as forceful as a jackhammer yet far quieter.

My head felt like it was swinging back and forth in a badminton contest. (Funny how such thoughts came back to me. Badminton? When had I last seen people playing badminton? Certainly not since my one-way ticket into space.)

"I told you she would become a Priestess," Tessa told Tem, not the least bit intimidated by the Westlan leader.

"Yes," he said. "I remember. And you are always right. I admit it. Shaara must be tested right away. Tomorrow, if possible. Then, inducted into your group before nightfall. It is not safe to allow an untrained priestess to wander at will."

Tenor bolted up. "She trains there, yes. But she stays with us — and with her children."

Tem shook his head. "That cannot be. Priestess candidates reside together. They do not mingle with others. It is too dangerous for them and for the rest of us."

I stood up. I knew my bondmates would fight Tem and Tessa. They had already told me they'd die for me. I couldn't allow them to get on the wrong side of the head of Westla.

"I would like to train with Tessa and the other Priestesses. There is a lot I don't understand about the Power, but I will not leave my bondmates. I am theirs, and they are mine," I said, using the words that Thedar had said earlier.

The cackle woman was back. Tessa practically fell out of her chair; she was laughing so hard.

31

"I like this new Shaara. She deserves to be the Queen of Altar."

Tessa hadn't disputed my words, but she hadn't approved them either. I looked to Tem.

"Who owns this woman now?" Tem demanded. "Shaarvan has left her with another. Who husbands her? I do not see Stegthal in this group. Has he passed on?"

I suppose that Spelon should have stepped forward then, claiming me as Shaarvan would have wished, but instead, Thedar cleared his throat and began the saga of Thal and his brutality.

Spelon's hand clenched more tightly around mine. He tugged me back down, then leaned over and kissed me. "Tem is stalling," he said. "He knows who comforts your nights. He has observed, if not mind dug for surety. Be at ease, my Shaara. We will soon get through this."

I tuned out their conversation then. Spelon was right. It was what Thal used to call *a time fritter*, a trivial side bar when the important things were still needing solutions.

At last, Thedar finished relaying the sequence of horrid events, but again, Tem returned to his question, not letting it go. Spelon pushed up from his chair and pulled me up so we were standing together.

"We have given you all the information you have asked for, Head of Westla. You know that Shaarvan seconded me. If Shaara were not Priestess, I would have rights to her, but as Tessa will tell you, a Priestess is owned by no male. She is free. We three bondmates still honor our pledge to shield her and the children. And as Thedar said, at night, Shaara will be under our protection."

I leaned into Spelon. Thedar and Tenor joined us, their shoulders side by side with ours. Once more, Shaarac was in my guardian's arms, and Thaandar had been handed back to me. Our small group must have appeared to be united against all of the mighty Westlan. Perhaps we were as insane as Thal.

Tessa nodded and stood as well. "Yes, this works. Her bonds to Shaarvan are glowing cords, throbbing with pain but still thick with the Power of the Saberey. But the four of them also have heavy vines that connect them strongly. The neophyte's, Tren, he was called, leaves an anchor behind that pains the girl. But he must stay with Shaarvan, restoring the Westlan heir, soothing the blister to his pride. I can see the stub of Stegthal's vine as well. It is broken, festering like a chopped-off limb. We must heal that. Such a pity, but it was his fault, not the girl's.

"Give them an abode, Tem. They must remain together. Convention is merely an unchallenged belief. This girl has no malevolence in her. She will do no harm to your citizens. Tem. More the pity, perhaps," Tessa cackled.

She nodded to Tem, her only homage to his position. "And as you wish, oh, Great One," Tessa said in a mocking manner. "I will arrange for testing tomorrow. But it is superfluous. Shaara is a Priestess. I can see the Power burning inside her. I know you see it as well.

"But let us dispense with further drama. These Shapechanger are tired from their travels. The children need rest and a safe place to lay their heads. Give them an abode, Tem. And funding, suitable to their position."

Tem's face remained impassive. For a moment, he stared at Spelon, then Thedar and Tenor. At last, his gaze moved to mine.

"Shaara, daughter of Trendacons, holder of the Power of the Saberey. I accepted you before as the wife of Shaarvan. Should you test out tomorrow, I will renounce your position as his wife."

"No!" I cried out.

Spelon jerked, reached out again for my hand, and gently squeezed it.

If Tem even heard my cry, he ignored it and continued. "I accept the children you have brought to us. They will be invested into the Westlan annals and tested as soon as their age permits."

Tem's eyes, green in Shapechange mode, speared us with his Power. "Thedar, Tenor, and Spelon, you are now under the Umbrella of the Trendacons and henceforth known as family. All resources of the Trendacons are given freely to you, and you may take up residence in the housing of the Trendacons. Suite West D should meet your needs, for it contains adequate space for your entire group."

He nodded to each of us and then to Tessa. Formalities over, his eyes shaded back to gray. They were rain clouds, dark and ominous at times but always scary. I remembered how panicked I'd been the first time when Shaarvan had brought me to him. My fear was no less now. Power, thick with threat, is nothing to take lightly.

"I will send for you at the appropriate time of Shaara's testing tomorrow," Tem said. "Shaara is to be accompanied by all of you, including the little ones, but additional guards will, from this point on, reinforce your family's protection."

Tem clicked his fingers, and eleven males sped over to his side. Tem pointed to seven of them. They reassembled behind us. The other four reformatted behind Tem.

"Thedar," Tem said, meeting the Shapechanger's eyes. "I thank you for the background on Stegthal's descent. His needs will be accommodated. Guards: Swen, Towen, Stept, see to Stegthal. He is still on their ship. Locate him and remove him. Remember that he is a Shapechanger Lord and Warrior. Be gentle with your control of him, but do not allow him to go elsewhere or to remain on the ship. Take him to the *Facility* where his mind can hopefully be restored."

"Starloft, show Spelon's group to their new chambers. Starloft will be the one to come for you at the appropriate time for Shaara's testing tomorrow.

"Satisfied, Tessa?" Tem asked, turning around to look back at her. She held up her hand and blew Tem a kiss in an almost flirtatious manner, then nodded with a huge, beaming smile.

Spelon took it upon himself to thank Tem for his kindnesses. Then we all nodded our heads for Tem and for Tessa and turned to leave.

"No," Tessa cried out in sudden anger, then turned to glare at me. "You will not fake your tests tomorrow, Shaara."

Mind reading Shapechanger were a pain. I gritted my teeth and avoided Tessa's glare.

Spelon looked down at me, apparently not understanding exactly what had caused Tessa's uproar.

But Tenor, quiet Tenor, picked up the gauntlet. "If you want Shaara to succeed, then do not steal her name and position."

"Oh, rubbish. Tem will not," Tessa said. "He cannot. Shaarvan and Shaara are Saberey bonded. He knows that. Nothing but death can sever their cords. Tem only meant he would give Shaara a formal designation as being a Priestess," she told Tenor.

"Shaara, you must promise me to do your best tomorrow. Do you hear me?" Tessa insisted.

I was still unsure about what Tem had meant, but I nodded to Tessa. I figured she'd work it out with him. She seemed to have a very good relationship with him. I wondered if his wife, Temina, knew (or cared?), but that was none of my business.

We had already been dismissed. There was no reason to linger. Tenor's statement had put them on notice, but it had also rattled

Spelon. He was so busy worrying about what I'd said he forgot to shift into the Warrior position. No matter. The seven guards Tem had gifted us with seemed more than adequate.

# *Chapter Four*

## Tenor

What a fine mix of praise and bullying. To be accepted into the family of the Trendacons was an honor. I had been rather envious of Tren for having that stroke of luck. But now I saw that such a declaration came with handicaps. We would be under the eyes of the government, weights tied to our shoulders. But as I had told Shaara, every reward carries a penalty. Would it be worth it? Yes.

We had gotten our wish to remain with Shaara. Perhaps, as Tessa had said, on Altar, Shaara was to be a Queen. That seemed fitting. Already, we revolved around her. Or, as Thal once explained, "She is our star, and we are driven to turn in her direction. She has become a basic need like air and water. She is now the source of our life force."

I had not understood Thal at first. He had seemed overly philosophical and dropped wisdom as if he were seeding a garden. We had learned to respect his knowledge and recognize his many gifts until he turned on Shaara.

Before becoming one of her guardians, Shaarvan had come to me with his proposal, and I had laughed in his face. I had been like the many listless Shapechanger youths who wandered about Westla, desiring something to clasp onto. I had been much older, of course, and I never would have sought to steal a female from her lord, but I was drifting the same as those young Shapechanger. Unanchored and more or less lost.

I had come to Westla for some kind of purpose Passes earlier. I needed a way to fulfill my life, although I had no idea exactly what that would be. Not in a sexual sense. Shapechanger could always find willing partners, pay for one or buy a girl.

I had thought before that point, before Shaarvan approached me, that my need was for allegiance to a cause, or in his case, allegiance to his family. So, I had agreed that I would guard and protect his wife and child.

But then I learned what I had not known. Allegiance was good, but it was family I needed.

That was why we, guardians of Shaara, were forced to be battle-ready when we walked about Westla. West was not a violent place. No murders, no battery, no break-ins, but the young needed something in the same way I had needed it. They had no idea what it was they were seeking. But they were drawn to Shapechanger females.

And Shaara would be the biggest draw of all. She was a compulsion they didn't understand because she contained all the elements they needed: beauty, Power, smiles, tender-hearted conversations, and that key component — the origin of family. The poor lost souls would think they followed her for sexual reasons, but there was more to it. They hungered for what they did not have and could not get.

Steghal used to say that *comprehension of self produces wisdom.* If so, I was at the very beginning of it. But Shaara was its key. I knew that. Shaara and her sons. My family.

That Tide, heading for the place that would be our new residence, we saw no wandering youths eager to engage us in battle. Probably due to an addition of seven pipe-carrying Shapechanger males, our trip was made swiftly and uneventfully.

As we entered the quarters we'd be given, the luxuriousness of it did not even touch my mind. I was too entwined with Shaara. Her body was leaking sorrow. Darn Tem and his officialness.

The moment the older child stepped through the doorway, her shoulders softened, and the immense stress she always seemed to carry of late caved in on her. She sat down on the couch, bowed her head, and wept, but it was the relieving kind of tears. Quietly, we stepped around her, explored our new surroundings, and situated the boys. One room already had a crib for Thaandar and a small bed for Shaarac. It was obvious Tem had planned the suite for us all along. So why had he prolonged the meeting?

Spelon sat down with Shaarvan. He was giving her the proper support. Change was difficult, but I figured that the four of us should be experts by now. I sought the biggest bedroom, which, of course, would go to Spelon and Shaara, backed out, chose a smaller room for myself, and then located Thedar.

I sat in his room for a moment. He was musing over the time we'd spent with Tem and Tessa. "That was something," he said.

I laughed. *Something* pretty much summed it up.

# Tren

For a place in the midst of war, Altar, from space, did not look damaged in any way. The greens of trees were still heavy, intermixed with various bodies of water. Even the nearest city, I saw as we flew over it, seemed untouched by bombs or missiles.

We were hovering over Space Port before I knew it. Three ships were ahead of ours, but Shaarvan told me that ours took priority, so we zoomed downward without much of a wait time.

Once we landed, I saw signs that things were not completely free of strife. Shaarvan had ordered guards for us, and when we stepped off the ship, I saw that *guards* didn't mean five or six, but a whole platoon of soldiers — an enthusiastic fifty or so individuals, all with pipe rifles at the ready.

As we set foot on the ground, I suddenly understood why it might not be safe for Shaara to come to Altar. Shaarvan had kept telling us so, but I suppose I thought his words were only an excuse.

A pilot car waited for us. We climbed in and soared upwards almost at once. The pilot noted that we were being followed, but Shaarvan recognized the vehicle as being "one of his."

When we landed, I got to meet the beautiful and loving Teea. She knew almost nothing about me, but she threw her arms around me and hugged me close. "You're the one who saved Shaara. I can't thank you enough. Welcome to the family. But where is my daughter?" she asked, turning to Shaarvan.

I was glad I did not have to be the one to explain. Teea's face was storm clouds and thunder.

I was given a room and told that this was my new home. I had zero complaints about that. It was a house like nothing I'd ever seen before. "Old Terran," Teea later told me. That reminded me again of Shaara. I remembered how she'd talked about playing card games at the table, how the couch had a texture like it had small pebbles in the fabric, and that the backyard was someplace where one could raise landoors.

Sure enough, when I checked it out, I envisioned something I'd never have thought of without Shaara's words. I could almost see Crimson Black galloping about a fenced-in section of it.

I was not planning on building a casino on Altar, at least not like the one I had owned on Freinana. Shaara would want to visit, and I would be uncomfortable with the riffraff that spent their time inside. If Shaara was going to return to Altar, which I was determined to make happen, even if she was only my little sister, I didn't want her around that.

And then there were the two little ones. Yes, probably no casino for me. I had sold the one in Freinana, so I would need to look around for something else to tend to. I certainly had sufficient funds for any business I wanted to invest in. Only I did not know how to do much of anything else.

Surveying the grassland that extended as far as I could see, I vowed to sit down with Teea and talk about an idea that had suddenly sprung into my head. I knew Shaarvan would not approve, but . . .

# Shaarvan

I was right about my mother's reception to what I had done. She was as bad as Tren. I was lectured clear until dinner. In the past, she never would have done so, but things were different now. I saw that. Females had "gained their own," to quote my mother. I guess that meant that she was free to criticize my treatment of my wife.

While being lectured, I drifted to my father's room. To my great disappointment, I found Tevor exactly the same as when I left. He did not react to my presence either by Mind Power or by facial expression. In fact, I could not tell if he was still in the body lying in his bed.

"I am back," I said, just in case. "Shaara is a Priestess now. She killed Thenos. So, if he was the one who did this to you, your revenge has been dealt in full measure. I would have preferred to do it myself, but Shaara has always been difficult, as you remember. Just like your wife, Teea. Come back to us, Father. I ask this for myself, for Teea and for Altar. If you can, come back. We need you."

Whether my father heard any of that, I do not know, but when I turned, I saw my mother. "We had heard that Thenos was dead, but not the details."

My mother's face was full of tears and held the lines of worry she had been enduring. She was much younger than my father, Tevor, but she showed a few signs of aging, mainly in the gray streaks of her hair. But they suited her. She was still a pleasing Shapechanger female. If my father had not already assigned another to Second her, others of nobility would be stepping forward.

Unaware of my thoughts, my mother continued. "Killing like that must have been very painful for Shaara. Is she all right?"

Her words startled me. I was proficient at hiding my thoughts, but I blinked from the surprise of her musings. I had not thought from Shaara's viewpoint. I had not wanted to see it.

A door opened inside my mind. Enlightenment. I had never thought how killing a person might hurt Shaara. I was fully aware of how tender-hearted she was. She was still innocent in so many ways, even after Freinana. Perhaps she had even been in shock after such a grievous act. And had I given her a moment of assurance or soothed her angst and guilt?

No wonder Tren had berated me for my cruelty. I had been harsh with my diminutive wife. I had spared no thought to her feelings. Could I not have sent her away in a gentler manner?

And yes, Tren was right. I had been a stubborn fool, caught up in my own malignancies. If I ever saw Shaara again, I would apologize. She had not deserved my vilification. I had only meant to sever us. To push her into going where she wanted to go, where she now needed to go. Did no one see that?

I said nothing of that to my mother. I left her to her grief and her evening's conversation with Tevor. Then I repaired to my room, which was blissfully free of Tren's accusations of Shaara's mistreatment. I had no doubts that it was all well-deserved, even more so now that I realized how short-sighted I had been, but I could simply not hear another word of it. My guilt cup overflowed.

Crawling into bed, alone, as I had been these Passes, I journeyed to the forest where my cottage used to be before Thenos burned it down. Dreams are supposed to refresh us, to soothe away the badness of a Tide gone wrong, or at least to better organize plans and decisions for the future. But not that sleep-cycle.

I spent my dreams with the Saberey, prowling at their side. But, like with my mother's disapproval, harassment seemed to come from all sides. The Saberey tigers attacked me for the first time ever. The big leader, She-Cat, raked my face with her claws, calling me a Worthless Prey, the worst insult of the Saberey.

Then, as if they were in a line-up, the others took their turns scratching and biting at me until I retreated, pulling myself out of my nightmare to find myself in bed, drenched as if I had fallen into Ragden Pond.

The Saberey were bristling with anger because I had sent Shaara far away again. They wanted her to join their hunt, to feel at one with them again. They wanted to get to know our sons, they told me.

It is true that the Saberey have tempers just as we do. They have special pets, too, those watched over, pampered, and adored. I used to be the preferred one. They worked with me, educated me on their beliefs, and accepted me in the tribe, but apparently no longer. Shaara was their darling one now. Lately, it seemed that Shaara was everyone's favorite.

I suppose that was not surprising. The Saberey had loved Shaara from the moment I brought her to Altar. They had guarded her during her Saberey transition and made her part of their pack. She had even given birth in their forest. Shaarac would one day hunt with them and join them in their play. According to what I'd learned in my dream, they accepted Thaandar, too. That was good.

But they had made it known that I had robbed the Saberey of both cubs and tigress. It was no wonder that I appeared to be their enemy. I was not allowed to explain. Excuses were not actions. I could restore my position with them only by bringing her with me to the forest.

But I would not be able to do that. How could I when she must live in Westla and I in Altar? I doubted she would ever return here. I would forbid it, for one thing, knowing the Commoners' intentions to steal her away and place her on that silly throne of theirs. Perhaps, one Tide, my sons could come, and I could take them to the forest. The Saberey might forgive me then or not.

But why was it that no one understood that what I did was for Shaara? I sent her to safety. After she became a Priestess, I sent her to Westla for training. Does everyone believe that I love her any less than before? How could that be possible when my heart would always beat to the rhythm of *Shaara, Shaara, Shaara?*

# Shaara

I really didn't understand why I was sobbing. I'd thought I'd given up my tears, yet here I was, sinking back into what my guardians were probably calling *my childish ways*.

But Tem's words kept looping in my brain. It was everything I didn't want to hear. He'd given up on Shaarvan loving me again, and I absolutely refused to believe it. Was that the reason for my tears?

Deserting Thal, knowing that guards would be escorting him off to some institution where strangers would disturb his research and his mode of operation: piled-high books, telescopes pointed at vital spots, his papers strewn across a desk, in some strange order that only he could figure out. It was the final straw of cutting ties. Guilt attacked me. I knew I'd betrayed him.

Then, there was the approaching test. The thought of it terrified me. I remembered too vividly the four tests that Shaarvan had forced me to take. The judgmental eyes peering down at me, the skeptics, the nature of what I'd had to endure. Whatever test the Priestess Guild threw at me, it would probably be even worse.

Yet, on the good side. Tem had not been angry that I'd killed his nephew. He hadn't said a word about that or how I'd had to disobey Shaarvan to do so. Tem hadn't rebuked me for taking the potion either. (Did he know that the Priestess potion was an illusion, something made up only to impress Shapechanger males?)

And why hadn't Tem punished me for drinking it? Did the Shapechanger believe that the production of Priestesses was a positive or a negative thing? Tem had urged Shaarvan to limit my instruction with Tessa, and he'd even discouraged my testing. Was it possible that tomorrow, he would sabotage my trial? If so, how?

My tears stopped, and I became aware that Spelon was trying to get my attention.

"Shaara," he said. "It will be alright. You need to eat now, then rest."

Males always thought that eating, sleeping, and sex would solve all problems. I smiled. It was possible that males were right. Those actions did seem to solve a great many difficulties or at least halt them temporarily.

# Spelon

I chose her favorite dish from the food processor. She nibbled on it in her dainty way. Her small teeth chewed a bite that I would have gobbled down in half the time that nibble took her. But that was her nature. I said nothing. I consumed my portion, drank my fill, and then waited for her to finish.

"The boys are okay?" she asked, knowing what I'd say.

I told her anyway. "They are asleep, Shaarac in a small children's bed and Thaandar in a crib. The suite is well fitted for us. Thedar and Tenor are probably resting in their quarters, as well. I plan to share your room. I assume that is acceptable to you?"

She pushed her food away. I hoped she'd consumed enough for her nutritional needs. It always surprised me how little she ate, but then her body was a great deal less weighty, her muscles less massed, even with the frequent workouts I ran her through.

"I would like that," she said. "May we check out our new bedroom now?"

I grinned, and she matched my smile. Taking her hand, I led her on our first exploration.

# Shaara

On Earth, there was an old expression. "A tiger can't change its spots." That wasn't true about Shapechanger in any sense. Spelon was not the bondmate he'd been before. He'd mutated into an intelligent male, one who was attempting to be aware of my desires and needs. I don't mean sexually. Spelon, like all Shapechanger, could attune to a female's body. Webbing, touching, or licking supplied them with everything they needed to know in terms of pleasing a woman.

But what I meant is that Spelon was adapting. No longer gruff and judgmental all the time, he was more intuitive than I'd ever believed possible. He asked instead of demanding. He sought my contentment rather than forcing his preferences on me. He was everything one could desire. Except he wasn't Shaarvan.

My deepest fear was that I'd send Spelon off the deep end into Crazyville as I had with Thal. Preventing that would be one of my first questions for Tessa. It was something I'd need to work on.

# Tenor

We were summoned early. We had finished eating our first meal of the Tide. Shaarac had just been hosed down after his bout of careless spilling. Thaandar had received his bottle and had his baby pants cleaned out and adjusted, and Shaara was looking calmer and more relaxed than I would have believed possible. It was a good morning. Then we felt a Shapechanger at our door and knew that it was time for Shaara's test.

Without comment, we rose and set out. Shaara's shoulders bowed once more from stress. Spelon became grouchy as a *biggleboo,* and the guards who followed seemed heavier than usual with their display of armaments. The thud of their boots against the path toward the Judgment Hall seemed an ominous threat.

We were not eager to arrive, but I think it was better to get it over with. Whatever the outcome, I knew that Shaara would feel less tense afterward.

I tapped her mind at one point. She was concerned about Tem's cheating. Would the head of Westla do that? Would he cheat for Shaarvan, his nephew, or for the good of Westla? I sent the concern I read in Shaara's mind to Thedar and Spelon. Both seemed surprised by the thought. But we were all neophytes to Westlan politics. We must be prepared for anything.

The Hall of Judgments was closed to petitioners that Tide. We walked into an empty chamber. Good, I decided at first. That would make it easier on Shaara. But then I thought about the possibility of Tem cheating, and I wasn't so sure.

A moment later, a group of Priestesses entered. All of them were old women. Tessa was not among them. Not good. Did Shaara truly belong with this horde of witchy old women?

My anxiety lessened when I saw Tem and Tessa enter from a separate doorway. I guessed that meant that everyone had arrived. Let the good times roll. (An expression we'd all picked up from Shaara. Her eyes sparkled appealingly whenever we said it.)

"Thank you for your presence here this morning," Tem said without waiting more than a moment to check that we'd brought the children, which, of course, we had. Where else would they be?

Tem called to a servant woman who scurried forward, the same one from the Tide before. She immediately reached out to take Thaandar from Thedar. Another female strode forward and showed Shaarac the toy she carried. Entranced by such a wonder, it was not difficult for her to lead the boy off to the side. Shaarac hadn't even asked permission to depart from our midst. We will be speaking to him later about that.

"Guardians," Tem said, "You must sit there," he said, pointing to a set of chairs.

There were three of us and about twenty chairs. Somewhat puzzling, but Thedar and I did as we were asked. Spelon remained by Shaara's side.

"I do not wish to be separated from Shaara," Spelon said stiffly, his body unbending in his Warrior mode.

"It's okay," I heard Shaara whispering to him. She patted his arm like she was the one in charge.

I smiled, but perhaps it wasn't that far off from our new reality. A person who could kill with a thought was not a weakling needing overt protection. Maybe in her own way, Shaara was now taking care of us as much as we were tending to her.

Spelon was obviously still pondering the situation, wavering since Shaara seemed to want him to go sit in the chairs as Tem had ordered. Perhaps Spelon also got a good look at the horde of Priestesses wrinkling up their noses as if they were ready to turn his manly parts into a soft mushroom. (Although, I'm pretty sure that some of them had a certain glint in their eyes that told me they wanted to make use of Spelon's parts in a much more conventional manner — those brazen witchy crones. Like he'd even glance their way since Shaara shared his bed.)

"Spelon, we are not removing her from your sight, silly Warrior. You may guard her equally well from a few steps away," Tessa informed him, grinning widely.

Apparently, the combination of orders, frowns, loving pats, and mockery convinced Spelon. Crossing his arms tightly enough that his muscles bulged twice as huge, he marched over to the chairs and sat down, his eyes still focused on Shaara.

Our girl had not been invited to sit. She didn't seem to mind. She was watching the Priestesses stack candles all about the room. Every niche was filled with a rainbow of colors, all of the candles with wicks untouched by flame. The steps up to the stage where Tessa and Tem were sitting were also decorated, all of them with squatty, fat purple candles. A chubby white one was placed on a chest-high podium the Priestesses had brought in, especially for the test. The white candle had delicate gold etchings that probably represented something to the mob of old hags. To me, the designs only looked decorative.

When the candles had all been neatly placed, the servant girls scrambled to exit from the hall. Then only Shaara, the Priestesses, the judges, and we three were present. It seemed that during the candle placement, Thaandar and Shaarac had been taken elsewhere.

I started to complain, but Thedar nudged me silently. "Tem will not allow them to come to harm. He is the boys' uncle."

"So was Thenos," I grumbled, sounding exactly like Spelon on a bad Tide.

Spelon glared at us, probably for talking. But hadn't he noticed the disappearance of the boys? Probably not. His eyes were fixated on Shaara.

"We begin now," Tem said.

Tessa stood. She sprouted some *mumble jumble* (another Shaara expression that had amused us, except when we'd been trying to discipline her.)

The Priestesses muttered the phrases in an echo of voices. The room dimmed and then grew dark. Magic filled the air. It felt itchy and smelled like the bread Shaara once burned, sending us all out of the Deadstar house to wait for the odor to become bearable.

Then we heard the phrase we'd all become accustomed to: "A Priestess lights candles," Tessa said. "Prove yourself, Shaara of Shaarvan, Shaara of the Trendacons."

"The test is only the lighting of candles?" Shaara asked, puzzled.

The group of harpies sneered. Tessa hushed them. "That is all you must prove, my dear. It is enough to prove your essence."

Shaara nodded. "Okay."

She closed her eyes. It took her much longer to produce her mind's candle lighter than it had ever done on the ship. I wondered if it was true that Tem had done something to affect her Powers. But before my unease could become any larger in my imagination, the white candle flared, as did every other candle in the entire hall.

"What!" one of the Priestesses cried out. "She wasn't supposed to do that. Those were new candles, never used. Now she has . . ."

"Quiet," Tessa shrieked.

She gazed down at Shaara. "Were you showing off, child?"

Shaara looked around at the Priestesses, then back at Tessa. "But I asked you. You said to light the candles, so I did."

Tem began to laugh. "No question, Shaara. You lit them all. Every last candle."

Tessa chuckled a moment, shaking her head. "All right, Child. Put them out."

"You want me to extinguish every candle, right?"

"She can't, I bet," said a cantankerous woman from the group. "And she has ruined all our new ones. They . . ."

"Hush," Tessa ordered again, eyeing the one who'd spoken.

"Yes, Shaara. Put out every candle."

Shaara shrugged, closed her eyes, and thought them out. She had snuffed out every candle without sputter or smoke. She even returned the wicks to their former unlit whiteness.

"Not possible," said one of the Priestesses. "It's a trick."

"No matter. She's too young. We don't take babies into our training facility. Let her grow a bit. Let her remain with the Shapechanger lords until she . . ."

"No, she passed the test," said another.

"It's a trick," repeated someone else. "The candles were never lit. You can see that. They are still . . ."

The bickering broke out into a riot of voices, all blending into unidentifiable jabber.

"Tessa," Tem said, breaking through the mishmash of argument. "Has Shaara passed the test? Does Shaara qualify as a Priestess?"

Shaara was looking lost. I knew that at any moment, she might either dissolve into tears or blast everyone with her temper. I stood up and took a step in her direction.

Tem saw and shook his head. "Sit," he thundered.

But Spelon and Thedar agreed with me. They both shot up to retrieve our wearied darling.

"Yes, she has succeeded. Shaara is a Priestess," Tessa declared. "Take her, Guardians. Bring her to me tomorrow. We will begin training. But where are her sons?"

As if they'd been listening, the two females returned the children the moment Tessa asked the question.

I grabbed the boy and Thedar the baby. Spelon went for Shaara. Without speaking to the still bickering priestesses, Tem or Tessa, we six swept out of the great hall as if lightning were chasing us.

# *Chapter Five*

## Shaara

To say that the testing was anticlimactic was an exaggeration. As far as I was concerned it had been a giant flop. If all they'd needed was one little candle lit, I could have done the test in my sleep. I'd reached inside a man's brain and cut off his synapses. I'd ended his life in a heartbeat. I'd . . .

Never mind, it was over, but the group of witches — as Tenor called them, and the term seemed to fit amazingly well — were even more disappointing. I wasn't sure I actually wanted to join in their midst. If those bickering old women were well-trained Priestesses, maybe I was better at exploring my Powers on my own. Of course, I wouldn't dare say that to Tessa. She was the exception.

My guys didn't act thrilled with the whole morning either. They'd been sentenced to chairs, out of the way, yet ordered to attend. For what purpose? How had their presence changed anything? Why had Tem required them to attend? And why bring the children when they were only going to be transferred to babysitters?

I had worked myself up into a tea kettle of hissing by the time we reached home. Spelon calmed me down with a bottle feeding for my cute little Thaandar, who giggled up at me the whole time. That was always a sure fix for a bad mood. Thedar and Tenor took Shaarac off to the backroom to discuss how he'd gone off with a stranger without getting an okay first. I guessed it would be a quick scold, though, because none of us had the energy for much more.

"How about a trip somewhere?" Spelon asked when we were all united again over food processor meals and drinks.

"I'm too tired," I said at first, but Shaarac started rooting for the zoo, which Thedar had told him about while we were still on the ship. (Good memory for a little kid, right?)

Anyway, I got talked into going by the *please, please, please* of my adorably dimpled son, and then it didn't sound like such a bad idea after all.

A zillion guards followed us about. (Well, maybe not that many, but at least seven.)

The zoo was the kind where the animals weren't kept in cages and instead lived in natural habits. There was greenery all around, lots of trees and flowers. It was a park with animals! I loved it. As did Shaarac. He was so excited; he was flitting about like one of the mini-kangaroo critters, which was the first exhibit we visited.

The animals were fun to watch. There were lots of babies who were frolicking about, play fighting, I think. Shaarac loved feeding a friendly, stubra-like, horsy creature. I can't remember what the plaque said the animal was called. There were also fish and turtle-like creatures sunning on the rocks. Except the turtle look-a-likes smiled at us. Turtles never smiled on Earth.

The zoo had more animals than Shapechanger visitors. Apparently the young Shapechanger males, who my Bondmates believed were a big threat to me, didn't care for zoos. All the other guests who were visiting that day took one look at my burly males and the guards who followed a couple of yards back and cautiously turned away to other areas of the zoo. We were left alone, a group of outcasts, highly contagious, obviously.

There was a play area for kids. It was well populated by family groups, but Spelon said it wasn't safe for us. Shaarac was about to protest with vigor, but Tenor suddenly suggested it was time to go get a treat, something delicious, like ice cream. My son looked back once at the children climbing up and down the various poles and rings, the tunnel for crawling through, and the massive push vehicles with wheels and horns that the children were noisily enjoying.

But Spelon, Shaarac's favorite bondmate, had been the one to say "no" to the playground, and Shaarac was enthusiastic about ice cream, so he wiped an eye, switched out Spelon's hand for Tenor's, and we moseyed along without any tantrum.

Spelon and I purchased (thumb-printed, actually, since Westla didn't use money) a popcorn bowl filled with tiny speckled sweetness. Shaarac wanted something different. He'd been promised ice cream. His choice was pink with brown stripes. What flavor it was, I have no idea, but he loved it.

His treat came not in a cone but in a wedge with an outer surface of, I think, a baked cookie. Triangular-shaped, the ice cream portion formed a sphere at the top, one that an adult would have demolished quickly, but Shaarac, easily distracted, was not speedy enough to avoid the drips. So, it proved to be a very messy snack, but with Shaarac, pretty much everything was.

He did the best he could to catch melty drippings, but the food stand was next to some animals that looked cat-like. A kitten (?) had been given a ball of yarn and was getting all tangled in it. Nothing dangerous; the kitty was having a ball. (Pun intended.) Unfortunately, this cat stole attention from the ice cream treat, and the drips grew numerous.

When Shaarac didn't want to hold the treat anymore and probably had more ice cream on his face and clothes than was left in the cookie wedge, we tossed what was left in a near recycle pot, then visited the necessary, which vacuum-laundered his clothes and restored him to pristine condition.

Meanwhile, while Shaarac was being mopped and polished, so to speak, I sat on a bench outside and gave Thaandar another bottle. While I was burping the baby, Thedar and Tenor took Shaarac off to a smaller play area, one no one else seemed to have found. Shaarac had a great time there, but his unsoiled clothing didn't stay clean long.

When Shaarac wore out, it was time to leave, but although Shaarac was yawning and slightly cranky from weariness, that zoo trip had been exactly what we needed.

Later. We all vowed to go on one outing every fiveTide. It was a great idea but plans like that don't allow for scheduling problems or turmoil. Sadly, we never returned to the zoo.

# Spelon

Thal, our former bondmate, the one who went crazy, beat Shaara up, and left her in a death spiral, broke out of the mental health clinic that evening. He was supposed to be in a facility that was completely secure and unescapable; at least, that's what Tem had told us. But Thal wasn't your average crazy person. He climbed through a screened and barred window, apparently using some kind of acid that melted the metal into liquid droplets.

We were just relaxing after a Tide spent at the zoo when a messenger came from Tem, informing us of Thal's escape.

The note we were given said that the trackers would find Thal quickly. Tem ordered us to stay inside and guard Shaara. (Like we didn't always make that our priority.)

I guess our faces were so horrified by the news of Thal's breakout that little Shaarac started crying. He was overly tired, it was true, but he rarely shed tears other than during his temper tantrums. Not even when Thal ignored him or when his brand new father, Shaarvan, took off on a ship without telling Shaarac goodbye had the little one cried.

The boy thought that only females shed tears, which was kind of our fault since we'd told him that. But it was also why his sobs were so startling to the rest of us.

Shaara tried to console him. Thedar played peek-a-boo, but even that didn't bring Shaarac out of his mood. Finally, Tenor took the little one into the other room and did a male-to-male talk with him. It seemed that Shaarac believed that Thal was going to come beat up his mother again. We all reassured Shaarac that we would never allow that. But how had Shaarac known? None of us had told him that Shaara's decline then was due to Thal.

Unfortunately, that was not the end of the drama that night. Not long after we put Shaarac to bed, a different messenger brought another note from Tem. This one said that we must go to Tessa's place because the guards had discovered an Altarian Shapechanger planting a sleep bomb in our backyard.

"If they've caught the guy, then why do we need to go anywhere?" Thedar asked.

Of course, no one had a response to that. We picked up the sleeping baby and Shaarac, who was too heavy-eyed to pay much attention and headed out. The seven guards Tem had given us streamed out in front and behind us, with several additional ones added, apparently due to the evening's increased threat.

The pathways through the halls were clear. No Shapechanger youths, no bomb-toting Altarians — at least none we noticed. We were almost to Tessa's when we spotted military guards all around us. Their pipes were drawn. Some had knives in their hands for single hand-to-hand, and others were wearing heat-seeking goggles.

Shaara was already trembling with fear, but she said nothing, just watched with eyes as wide as *gallick sterns*. I held my pipe at ready, preparing to push her behind me at any spot of movement, but the army of males retreated from us. It looked like they were chasing someone they'd seen dart behind a building.

I relaxed my shoulders visibly, wanting Shaara to think the peril was past, but my sense of danger remained on high alert. It was a night full of threats. My brain assessed blind corners, shadows, and strange shapes I had never noticed before. Of course, it had been Passes since we had gone this way. Anything could have been altered.

I could feel Thedar and Tenor at my back. The other guards, Tem's guards, were treading lightly and scanning the vista for menace. Such was our passage to Tessa's house, slow and torturous with lots of unresolved tension.

When we finally arrived, one of the guards knocked at the door, but this was Tessa's door. The High Priestess, full of Power and foreseeing, should not have needed our knock. Tessa would have known we were there unless she were unconscious . . . or worse.

We instantly backed against the wall of the building, Shaara in the center, holding the baby, Shaarac, at her feet. The boy looked fully awake and wide-eyed with fear, but he was Shapechanger. He made no sound, just stared out into the distance.

"It is Thal," Shaarac whispered.

That was startling. The child should not know. He was too young for Shapechanger Power, but his voice had been assertive, no question in his declaration.

"Daddy," Shaarac whispered, uncertain whether that was a good thing or a bad one. Shaara squatted down, placing a hand on his shoulder, still holding the baby in her arms. It was too much for her balance. She plopped down on the ground, pulling Shaarac closer, holding the baby against her bosom.

Thanks to Shaarac, we knew who the enemy was. But why were we out in the street if Tessa was not home? Why had Tem ordered us to leave the protection of our guarded residence?

The house was witch-locked, but one of Tem's guards broke us in. Good trick. I wanted to ask later how he did that. One would think that anything Tessa locked would stay locked. I assisted Shaara in standing up and took the baby from her. Tenor rushed in to grab up Shaarac. Then, as a group, I drove us forward, my pipe still at the ready, guards at our back.

Once inside, we called out. Guards searched the house, but Tessa was not waiting inside for us. Nor did we find her unconscious body lying in the halls. Apparently, she was elsewhere. At the Priestess institution? With Tem? But why had we been sent out into the night? Why had we been told to come here? Nothing made sense. Our night's excursion suddenly struck me as false. What if it hadn't been Tem who sent that note?

Shaara knew her way around the house. She turned on the lights and located a room where we could rest, and the boys could sleep. I sent a guard back to Tem to question him concerning his purpose in having us leave the safety of our residence. Also, I wanted to alert Tem to the possibility that Thal might be near. It was all we could do. We were not about to return to our abode. The night was darker than it should have been. Someone had blacked out all the street lights.

Thedar searched the house for weapons, but he returned shortly, having found none. That was not surprising. Normally, a Priestess of Tessa's level would have no need for physical weapons. While the guards prowled through the house, keeping watch over the entrances, the four of us remained in the room with the boys, waiting for morning or for information supplied by the return of Tem's guard.

I could see that Shaara was wilting from the zoo trip and her stress from her Priestess testing. It was possible that her use of Power had exhausted her as well. I did not really understand the source of such. Did it eat at a body's reserves?

But I knew that Shaara never slept well when tension mounted. It was something we had learned from our Passes on Deathstar, the moon, and on the ship. I told Shaara to close her eyes and lean into me. Wrapping a blanket around her that Thedar had found while searching for weapons, I covered my woman and massaged her back while sending calming thoughts into her mind.

"I won't sleep," she told me, but she closed her eyes and was dozing practically before she had gotten the words out. The gentle flow of her breathing grew regular. I admired her face for a moment, then resumed patrols with my eyes, although the only door to the room was guarded by Tem's guards stationed at alert.

The night was long. It was a stranger's house we were in. The different minute noises I heard, the threat from the outside, and the knowledge that Tem's guards, basically unknown individuals who roamed about the other rooms with their quiet tread — none of that allayed my caution but instead stimulated it.

While noting such things, part of my brain continued to analyze the night's occurrences. Thal used to tell us there were no single actions of happenstance. Everything was tied to something else in a chain reaction. He would usually dart into his astronomical parallels then, which I had mostly tuned out during his lectures, but I used Thal's strategy for placing events into a more precise order.

Thal had escaped. A bomber had been seen prowling about our residence. Had anyone captured him? The terrorist was Altarian, they had said, but how did they know that if they had not captured him? And why would someone from Altar want us dead? No, not dead. A sleeper bomb. So, they were after Shaara and possibly Thaandar. Tessa had said they viewed the baby as their Royal Prince.

Then, there was the note ordering us to leave the safety of our new dwelling. But that made no sense. We had thought so at the time. Leave the safety of walls to venture out into the dark of night? Of course, there had been lights then. The city of West always maintained well-lit pathways during the hours of rest. How had the bomber or Thal shorted out the lights?

And why had we been directed to Tessa's? Why not go, instead, to the Great Hall, where guards and soldiers were always in attendance? A whole army of Shapechanger harbored there, and spare rooms must be abundant in a place so massive.

And where was Tessa? Why was she not here? Old women did not usually stray from the warmth of their quiet quarters. They rested in chairs, read their books, and nodded off with a cup of *Cha*. Hadn't she had a pet? Where was the miniature Saberey cat that so often had yowled at us, displaying sharp-pronged claws and teeth with razored peaks?

Then there was the mystery of how Shaarac had said he sensed his father, Thal. It made sense that the child of two strong Power holders would develop early, but this early? Was that possible?

Shaarac had shown no fear of Thal as the boy had earlier when he had reacted to hearing of the Shapechanger's escape. Shaarac somehow had realized that Thal had hurt his mother onboard the ship, hurt her badly, in fact. Why had his fear of Thal been dispelled in the dark at an unknown corner while his mother trembled in fear, squatting down to pull him against her? The reason for that was beyond me unless Thal, himself, had sent out tendrils of calm to nullify the boy's fear.

But wouldn't we have felt that use of Thal's Power? None of us had sensed his presence. Even Shaara, who should have picked it up immediately . . . but then she'd been exhausted, warn out, desperately short on sleep. Was that the explanation?

So many riddles, and right now, the biggest one concerned the messenger I'd sent back to Tem. Why had he not returned? Had Tem held him there? Had the messenger been killed on his way to Tem?

Could there be a link between Thal and the bomber? They must be two separate occurrences. If they had been one and the same, we would have been told that, I presumed. Someone would have identified Thal. The guards knew him. They had delivered him to the facility.

Thal had broken out of a secured area with acid. How did he get the acid? Why was it that the guards had not prevented Thal's escape? Weren't those in a facility for the insane doubly guarded? Tem cared about the safety of his citizens. He would have provisioned it well. And a Shapechanger who had attacked a woman, one who was a Trendacons? No, too many gaping holes in the framework, as Thal in his saner Tides would have put it.

Could Thal have used outside help to break himself free? Someone from Altar who liked to set sleeper bombs? Had Thal switched sides and aligned himself with the Altarian Commoners? No. Not possible.

Aligned with Shaarvan, possibly, but that made no sense either. Shaarvan could have seized his sons or Shaara at any time. This could not have anything to do with Shaarvan.

More likely, the kidnapping of the children and Shaara was meant to cripple Shaarvan's war effort. No matter how angry Shaarvan was with his wife, he would not trade her life to save Altar. Or would he? He'd left the war to save her before. And himself.

But that was a moot point. If insurgents had intended to capture Shaarvan's family for such a purpose, they would have failed.

What had Thal been doing near Tessa's house? He would not need our help to find the dwelling. So why had he followed us? The fact that he had not taken us out meant that either he had not had a clean shot, or else he did not want to.

Of course, there were more than seven additional guards. I would guess an additional eight had been added that night, although more could have been hidden. But a Shapechanger who could escape a high-security facility must have the skills to . . .

Would Thal turn on us that way? Would he want his closest friends, his family, dead? I would have said before that Thal would never hurt Shaara, but look what happened. He was no longer predictable, no longer driven by the rational, so anything was possible.

My brain ran circles all about the sequences and connections logic. Perhaps such exercises in thinking aided Thal, but for me, it felt like head strikes against a stone wall.

All the events of the night seemed scattered like pebbles in a garden plot. Perhaps Shaarvan or Thal could have seen a progression that fit things together. Their brains worked that way. Mine, obviously, did not. All I'd achieved was an ache in my brain that forced me to close my eyes for a moment of self-healing. When I opened them again, I needed a longer restorative view of Shaara and the children to recover, but my stress remained, and my head continued to throb.

If only we understood what had happened to Tem and Tessa. We would know more then.

"Any thoughts?" I asked Tenor, whispering softly to avoid waking up the sleepers.

He shook his head and glanced at Thedar, whose shoulders lifted in puzzlement. So, it made no sense to any of us.

Tessa did not return to the house, nor did the guard we'd sent to Tem ever show up, but when morning came, we looked out and saw nothing alarming. The streets were clear. The army of males we'd seen in the night was apparently playing their wargames elsewhere unless they were part of all this, sent to find Thal or the bomber. But would they not have signaled to us? One of them would have stopped to update our knowledge, I would think. If the search were connected. If Tem had sent the soldiers.

We ate a meal from Tessa's food processor. Shaarac was no longer fearful. He thought we were just having an adventure, as Thedar had told him. He laughed about being in Tessa's house. He'd seen her before and knew she was strange but not threatening.

The hour was late when a tramp of males pounded across the path, nearing where we were hiding. Tenor volunteered to meet them at the door. I hung back to be the boys' and Shaara's shield, although we had no cause to consider them in danger. Thedar chose to back up Tenor, but we were all practically defenseless, *sitting ducks*, as Shaara had explained to us, one Tide. We'd decided that it was a funny expression that meant absolutely nothing except that it brought a smile to Shaara's face whenever we said it.

The tromping boots halted at the front door. I heard the guards who had spent the night with us, guarding Tessa's domain as well as the rest of us, order Tenor and Thedar to back up. The guards met the soldiers at the door.

I listened, wondering if I should hide the children and Shaara, but it was too late. The soldiers had already entered. The crisp beat of their trod told me the path of their arrival. I rose with my pipe weapon, ready for battle, knowing that I had failed to foresee whatever was about to occur.

But it was Tem at the head of the platoon. He waved the soldiers back and entered the room, then sat at the table. Shaara stood up, ran to the necessary, and then sat beside him. They both smiled at Shaarac, who was climbing up on the chair and then at the baby who Tenor brought over.

"You are well, I see," Tem said. "It has been a busy night."

# Shaara

Shaarvan's uncle was becoming more and more irritating. I felt the urge to blast him with a siege of verbiage. Freinanan swear words might be most appropriate. But Thedar and Tenor were standing nearby, watching me. Their eyes held a warning, something that once would have sent me into a bowed head with signals of contrition but now only made me rethink and pull back on what might have made me feel a moment's satisfaction but would not be diplomacy in its purest essence.

Thedar took his verbal sword and attacked meaningfully. "I think you owe us an explanation for what we went through last night. You frightened the children and sent us on a wild chicken hunt."

"Wild goose chase," I corrected, then grinned, which is exactly what Thedar had intended me to do.

"Did Thal escape?" Spelon asked.

"Yes, I'm afraid so. We could not catch him, although we hunted him through the night. This morning, we found him dead. He had killed the bomber, though. Stegthal died protecting you, Shaara."

"My daddy is dead?" Shaara said in a tone of incomprehension. "Daddy was here. He watched over us. Now he is gone. Like Daddy Shaarvan gone?"

"No," I said, shaking my head with a sick feeling in my stomach for Thal's death. "Your father, Shaarvan, is on Altar. That's another planet. You will see him again when the war ends. But Thal . . ."

I almost got it out before my tears came. Spelon, as usual of late, anchored me. He was standing behind me, but he placed his arm across my shoulder to remind me that he cared. I could feel the love of the others as well. We shared that for a moment, feeling our mutual sadness. Thal had once been our friend and my husband for many Passes. If we remembered as he was back *before*, we could miss him.

Tenor took over what I'd begun. He picked up Shaarac and carted him off. He was whispering something. I could see from my son's face that the words were helping. I was blessed with the kindness of my guardians.

Tem still watched us. He licked his lips and asked for a drink. Thedar brought him a fruit drink, then sat down at the table.

"Thaandar looks healthy," Tem said, admiring my younger son, who was just finishing his bottle. Any minute, a smelly explosion out of his posterior would make the baby less appealing, but for the moment, he was gurgling with smiles. His rosy cheeks were plumply charming.

Perhaps an uncle should be the one to take him to the necessary room for cleaning, I thought, then smiled evilly. Thedar laughed out loud, then nodded, catching my thought.

That exchange was not something Spelon saw. He was a dog with a bone, and so far, it had not been chewed. "Where is Tessa?" he asked.

She was relocated to my quarters for the night," Tem said calmly. "I feared that Thal might wish to retaliate for her role in all this. Since Thal was located not far from here, it may have been a proper call."

"Then why did you send us here?" Spelon demanded, as angry as I'd ever seen him. A yellow haze shadowed the table. The rotten garbage smell of anger was so pronounced that, for a moment, I almost missed baby Thaandar's unlovely poop fragrance.

"Ick," I said. "Thaandar alert."

"Come, Tem. As his uncle, the honor is yours," Thedar said, laughing as his eyes met mine.

I handed the baby to Tem most eagerly. The baby's purges often spread his scent onto the one holding him. I was delighted to release him to Tem. It seemed fitting after our horrible night.

Tem held the baby at a bit of a distance, showing that either he found the odor as appalling as I did or else he knew all about the fluid contagion of such expulsions.

"One moment, Spelon," Tem said. "First things, first."

I giggled a moment but then suddenly remembered that Thal was dead. I think he would have appreciated my good humor. In fact, he always stopped to watch my laughter, saying he enjoyed the fullness of my joy. But it still wasn't proper. I should be mourning him. I should be subdued and despondent.

Since Shaarvan left, I'd had little discourse with Thal, but our chats when we'd lived on Deathstar and during our travels had shown me his wisdom. Almost a Pass of it. He had been a good teacher. We had been friends, lovers, and parents together.

And now, his death freed me. I would be able to recall my memories without fearing the threat of his violence and insanity. I wiped at a tear, but I didn't chide myself for showing emotion. Thal had praised tears as being the body's method of clearing out unhappiness. He would have appreciated my weeping over his death.

"Thal will always remain a part of us," Thedar said. "We can appreciate his insights now without the guilt of his betrayal of you, Shaara. We can move on."

Spelon shook his head. "I feel no sorrow for his death. He deserved to die."

Both of them were correct. His death did not make Thal a hero. But, as Thedar said, there had been good times. Thal showed us how to build the houses and how to construct a sewer so it didn't contaminate the water for our garden irrigation. He had made many level-headed decisions that had saved our lives. And now he was gone. Perhaps grieving was essential for those who lived, to clear away the sadness as my tears had so often done.

"Whatever you need, Shaara. We will lament his departure if you like or toss rocks at his telescope," Thedar said.

Tem was walking back into the room with a giggling Thaandar, thankfully, a clean-smelling, giggling Thaandar.

"That is correct. Basically, we will do whatever makes you feel better," Tem told us. "You will be in charge of that, Shaara, since he was your husband. We do not bury bodies or spread them in the sea, as was done on your home world, but we can prepare his body as it pleases you and send him out into space."

Space. Yes. I nodded. "Thal would like that. He once told me that he'd decided to wed a star. It was a good way to die, he'd said. It is too late to do so alive, but we can send his body into a star, can't we?"

"Yes, of course," Tem said. "Easily done, my dear. Do you others have thoughts on this?"

Tenor was probably still walking about the house with Shaarac, telling him stories about his father or perhaps playing a game of toss. Thedar and Spelon shook their heads in response to Tem's question. "When you're gone, you're gone," Spelon said. "It does not concern me. Only the present matters. Why did you tell us to come here, Tem?"

Spelon gave Thedar no chance to voice his opinion on how Thal's funeral should be handled or the best way to bid him farewell. But since the question Spelon had asked was probably at the front of all our minds, Thedar didn't stop the conversation from returning to the night's activities.

"I did not send you a note, "Tem said, rubbing his eyes. It was then I realized how tired he was. Apparently, the night had cost him sleep, too.

"Nor did I send a messenger to request that you journey out into the night when an Altarian sleep bomber and Stegthal were both on the loose. I would guess that note was from Stegthal. His last act was to save you from being captured. Even in his insanity, he still loved you, Shaara."

The details of the night slowly unfolded. It all made more sense then.

Tessa arrived just as we were heading out to return to our residence. "Where are you going?" she screeched. "It is time for training. Turn around and go back."

We'd had a tough night. None of us felt like dealing with Tessa, but we turned around and went back into her house.

"We had an adventure," Shaarac told her. "We ate your food."

The cackle woman was back. She scooped up Shaarac and hugged him. "Anytime you want, you are welcome to have an adventure at my house, little Shapechanger."

"He has Power on him," she suddenly exclaimed. "Tem, little Shaarac is another Shaarvan. I can feel it inside him already."

That was the good news. The bad news — the *additional* bad news was that my drills were no shorter for having been frightened and exhausted from our long night of what Shaarac called *an adventure*. The Power exercises were almost my undoing.

The males had taken Shaarac and the baby to a nearby park and were probably catching some sleep-eye with Tem's watchful guards in attendance. At least, I hoped so. But I needed Tessa's instruction, so I endured the brutal and seemingly unending torture.

Without my guardians defending me, at last, I had to pull the train cord myself in order to stop Tessa's nonstop assault. But strangely, instead of being disappointed or angry with me, she merely laughed.

"It's about time, girl. I thought you'd never plead fatigue. It's good to know you have at least a small measure of self-preservation and a backbone, even without those mighty Warriors looking like they'd like to tear off my ears for making you work hard."

As if she'd publicly announced the stoppage of my suffering, Thedar, Tenor, and Spelon were suddenly standing in front of Tessa's house.

But it wasn't until the moment I reached the door to our own suites, our new home, that I remembered that I'd forgotten to question Tessa about what worried me most. How did I stop Spelon from slipping into Thal's crazy? Tomorrow, I'd demand to know. I skipped dinner and dragged myself off to bed. Fatigue took me under the moment I laid my head on the pillow.

# *Chapter Six*

## Tenor

As Tides continued, I watched Shaara push herself through her studies with Tessa as if propelled by an inner compulsion. Had the impact of Thal's death been that severe that she must now hurl herself toward the edge of exhaustion, or was it her desire to return to Altar, where Shaarvan could once more kick her in the stomach with his rejection?

I discussed the subject with Spelon and Thedar. They, too, worried that her advance into Priestess knowledge was too fast. Could Tessa not see that Shaara was a young woman who still needed some fun in her life?

Shaara often played with the little ones. I heard her laugh when Shaarac did. With the baby she was down on the floor crawling with him or helping him to stand up. She watched as he took his first step. She was always a good mother, but now it seemed that her presence had become more duty than joy.

Our plan to make weekly trips of the sights of Westla had been tabled. Shaara said she could not afford the luxury of Tides off. We pleaded with her. It was not the first time I wished that we were able to order her to do something, and she would obey. Her stubbornness was ever-present.

It was with this scenario that I set off to visit Tem in what he called the *Great Hall*. His name for it, like his refusal to accept a regal name for his position, seemed beside the point. The obvious part being that he lived in a palace and was the king of Westla. But who was I to argue over such nomenclature?

I was hoping to appeal to his good sense. He was Shaara's uncle, after all, even if only in name. Surely, he cared enough about her to insist that Tessa lessen the girl's load.

I thought I would find myself in a long line of petitioners, but I had forgotten or misunderstood the value of being a member of the Trendacons family. The Shapechanger at the entryway recognized me at once and shuffled me forward. I had only to wait through the discourse of a youth requesting passage to an outward planet for a research project, which was granted, before I was called forward and stood before the Head of Westla.

Once he saw me, Tem removed himself from his throne, which was called *the Chair of Authority* or *the Chair of Judgement*, depending on the use of it during the rulings. Tem motioned me over to the side, where a grouping of four chairs were situated around a small table. He immediately called for some *Cha,* the hot drink everyone in West seemed to love but which I was not fond of. Without waiting any further, I set forth my case.

"Tessa works her every Tide?" Tem asked. "Have you spoken to Tessa about this concern?"

As if she would ever listen to a Shapechanger, I thought, although admittedly, Tem seemed to have broken through the woman's resistance to develop some kind of relationship. Shaara once said that the two were lovers, but Tessa was not one I could imagine Tem placing in that category. For one thing, Tessa was as old as the Priestess crones, who had bickered like youngling cats fighting over a toy. For another, she was crotchety and argumentative. But that was Tem's business, not mine.

"It is easy to become consumed," Tem said. "I, too, have the same problem, which is why I demand a Tide free each fiveTide. That allows me to resume my position with better concentration and greater enthusiasm for the needs of the citizens.

"I am sure Shaara will find that to be true once she follows such a program. But why is she not attending the Priestess Institute? Why is she still working only with Tessa?" he asked as he sipped his drink.

That was another matter that I had wondered about. Yet, it seemed of little importance if Shaara was getting the help she needed.

Tem finished his *Cha* then asked me if I wanted more. I shook my head. But when the serving girl returned with a pot of it, she refilled my cup despite the shake of my head.

"And you, what are you, Spelon, and Thedar planning to do on Westla? Have you decided on an area of interest?"

Tem leaned forward, studying me like my answer was of great interest to him. But we three Shapechanger were not high lords. We were from different planets with obscure, inconsequential backgrounds. Why should Tem care?

"Spelon is attending classes," I said. Thedar and I figured it was because he wished to become more like Thal, at least in Shaara's eyes, but I didn't reveal that to Tem. That was Spelon's business.

Thedar, like me, seemed uncertain about what this new position of ours meant and what our future would look like. But most important was that we did not know how long we would remain in Westla. I think the plan was to stay until the end of Altar's war and/or Shaara's completion of training, although I was sure that the first would outweigh the second.

"I think Thedar and I are merely waiting to see what the future holds. As you know, wherever Shaara and the boys go, we go."

A relaxed Tem, as he was in the faux wooden chair, his legs stretched out and his posture slightly slouched, was rather a revelation to me. Seeing him outside of his official capacity was like opening up a box and finding nothing more unusual than someone's used jacket.

Tem steepled his hands and leaned forward, his elbows perched on the table, further adding to his image of an average Shapechanger in relaxation mode.

"Yes, I thought as much," he said. "You three are loyal to Shaarvan, but I think, even more so to Shaara and the children. They are your family now, is that not true?"

I nodded, realizing that he saw more than I'd thought. Tem apparently understood about commitments and did not seem to think less of us for being at the dictates of a female.

"Then you will want an update," he added, straightening his body as if taking on the shawl of authority once more. "Shaarvan informed us that most of the Commoner troops have been eradicated, or at least have visibly withdrawn, perhaps to lie in wait in various hidden locations.

"The new government is being formatted as we speak, but the talks are not going smoothly. The Commoners, despite their evident defeat, are still insisting on certain demands. Both sides have agreed that the new Altarian government will be fifty percent Commoners, which I suppose is fair considering the nature of Altar's population.

"But the stickiest point is that the Commoners remain insistent on the return of their Queen and heir. They demand and will not accept alternatives. One of their mandates is that the Queen is to become the new head of the Board of Elders. Can you imagine a woman in charge of all Altar? The Commoners have stipulated that Queen Thenosa, our very young and newly made Priestess Shaara, must be installed before any formal agreements are signed.

"Shaarvan refutes that with endless legal babble, which is ignored. Although there is an abundance of evidence that Shaara was never Theno's wife, her reign on the throne has become the guiding principle of the Commoners, one they all rally for.

"According to Teea, Shaarvan has become a walking growl, his face shadowed in fur and his eyes as green as lichen." Even the mention of his wife sets him off into roars and tirades of rage. His brother Pathe no longer visits, and Tren seems unable to persuade Shaarvan to accept her back. It is a mess.

"As it stands now," there will be no official peace until Shaara returns to Altar to take the throne."

"What madness," I said, taking a sip of the tongue-nullifying drink I was supplied with. "Do you think Shaarvan will eventually yield and allow Shaara to return?" It was the number one question we guardians wanted to know.

If the war were at its end, would Shaarvan still demand that we leave Shaara behind on Westla and bring his sons to him? Of course, we would not. To tear a mother from her children? To separate us from Shaara? We could never do that, even if Shaarvan commanded it.

If Tem entered my mind to see my thoughts, he did not mention it, nor did his face display any displeasure at my resistance to Shaarvan's wishes. He simply nodded as if there was no question in his mind that the day would come when we all flew to Altar.

"Shaarvan will not discuss his wife either with his mother or with Tren. Shaarvan is old school. He believes the texts as they were written long ago cannot be amended. He refuses to acknowledge that all things change.

"And even though the Saberey and the Old Ones are equally adamant that Shaarvan must accept Shaara back as his wife, he remains wedged in his stubbornness." The Saberey tells me that it matters only that Shaara is a Trendacons. To them, her gender is not as important as her genealogy. I agree with them.

"Shaara is special. If Altar forces her to become their Queen, I believe that she will be a thoughtful and impartial one. According to Tessa, and from what I have observed, Shaara will bring positive change. I know she listens to you three and will take into consideration the views of the other Altarian Shapechanger, but she will also balance the rights of the Commoners with open-minded justice.

"Only Shaarvan refuses to admire her rise in Power or to see the good we see in her. The Power she holds is only at his beginning. Strange how much Shaarvan despises that but was the cause of it. Quite a quandary, I'm afraid. Even Tessa does not see the path forward yet."

The *Cha* had coated my tongue with its bitterness. I could not taste it anymore. I finished my cup, placed it down on the table, and prepared to leave.

"One other item," Tem said, noting my attempt to depart. "The Shapechanger who placed the sleep bomb at your house has been identified. His name was Chaslow, and he apparently worked for Thenos. It is theorized that he is the one who blew up the preschool, which killed twenty-three of Westla's younglings.

"Why Chaslow would still be after Shaara after Thenos' demise is still unknown to us. On Altar and here, researchers are trying to ferret out Chaslow's purpose. I suspect as I have all along, that the Altarian Commoners engaged him to seize Shaara and the baby. If that is correct, they will try again. We must all be watchful."

With that news, I found myself on the edge of an explosion. I closed my eyes and breathed in and out slowly, resisting the change rising up within me. Anger, or in this case, rage, was the Shapechanger adrenaline that surged our Sabereys into life. Although I was old enough to confine it, such a surge of Power still required considerable meditative control.

In Shapechanger society, Saberey's self-control was never mentioned. Tem merely waited for my Power to restabilize. Taking advantage of the moment, he waved for another cup of *Cha*.

When my full restraints were back, my fury at Tem's news lashed out with words. "Must Shaara spend her entire life hiding from Thenos' machinations?"

Tem watched as the servant girl again replenished his cup. I turned mine over so she wouldn't fill it again.

Tem sipped the hot liquid, sighed with pleasure, then looked up at me.

"When a mirror is shattered, it is impossible to restore it to its original form. We can only move forward as we are doing. Shaara will never again be the young, innocent Shaarvan brought to see me. She is altered and reformatted. Who is to say that she is not improved by these changes? Shaara has certainly increased her Power. Tessa says she is also finding her own backbone and growing in wisdom and strength.

"My nephew must learn to accept who Shaara is becoming, as Altar must accept its reformatting, even if that means with a Queen on their throne.

"My wife, Temina, before the madness sucked her under, had two favorite sayings: *Change is the only constant.* It was something said in her home world, but I think it is true with us, as well."

"And the other?" I asked for politeness' sake as much as for personal curiosity. Shaara had already told us that Temina's mind was unstable, and also that she had never transformed. The Head of

Westla's wife never becoming Shapechanger was an amazing revelation because Tem could so easily have discarded her and replaced her with another girl, one who could bear him children. Yet, he had not. He continued to care for her.

"Temina said something that, even when I was still young and rigid in my beliefs, changed my life. She said, "A person's soul is constructed on and by emotions.""

I could read Tem's face at that moment. His earnestness and the emotion of his memories were open to me. It was an amazing surprise to see — the leader of all Westla opening to an off-world Warrior whose fame existed solely in connection with Shaara. For a moment, the shock of it left me speechless.

Tem drained his cup, sighed, then put it down gently. "I think about those words often. It is the explanation for everything. It is why Shapechanger males are enhanced by the imprint of deep bonding. A woman's emotions empower us with their flood of feelings. I think my wife was right that emotion is what creates our souls."

He shifted his position, blinked, then brought himself back. It was as if, for a moment, he'd journeyed elsewhere, into untapped depths. Had I just peered deep into the source of Tem's great capacity for understanding?

Thal had once said that enlightenment came from within each person, but maybe it was possible to offer it to another when that person was ready to hear. I thought I might be ready, or at least I would try to be. Tem's flow of words had given me much to ponder.

But, I could not help wondering why Tem had initiated such an outpouring. Was he merely lonely, or was there a reason for his disclosures?

# Shaara

The next time my bondmates took me to Tessa, she rejected me, expelling me from her house as if I were a piece of trash that needed disposal. I could not tell whether she was angry at me or not. Her face was shuttered. Yet, she lectured Spelon, accusing him of being a poor caretaker. Poor Spelon. He tries so hard to fulfill my needs and then for Tessa to scold him like that. My anger flared.

Thedar grabbed me back, restricting my attack, but it did no good. I closed my eyes, manufactured a full bucket of water, then poured it over Tessa's head. It was the most potent magic I'd produced since I'd murdered Thenos. I felt a moment's pride, and then the backlash of my revenge hit.

"I'm sorry, Tessa. Please, please forgive me," I said, flashing the Shapechanger gesture of contrition.

Tessa looked a sight. Her hair dripped water down her front. Her clothes were fully saturated. The carpet beneath her might never be the same. I bowed my head and stood ready for her to launch her counterattack, but only her laughter came.

I looked up and saw that, with a wave of her hand, she had dried herself. Her hair, her dress, and the carpet looked the same as always. Only her face was altered. Her eyes were alight with satisfaction, and her smile was so full, I saw the woman she must have been when she was young.

"You are ready," she said, cackling as of old.

"Tomorrow. No. A Tide off for fun, then you report to the Priestess Institute. In a twoTide, you become one of us."

"See to it, Shapechanger Spelon," Tessa said, meeting Spelon's eyes.

Tessa turned and walked back into her house, leaving me gasping for breath. The magic had not tired me, but the abruptness of the morning's change left my lungs shy of breath.

"There," Tenor said, which made no sense. I turned to stare at him, scarcely needing air for that. His expression was not poker-faced at that moment. It was full of an almost haughty smugness, which was entirely unlike him. It was as if he thought he'd created the recent scene. And the others' faces displayed similar complacency.

For a moment, I thought that I should investigate, but then I remembered I had two full Tides off. I darted over to Tevor, who was holding the baby, and tickled my son's belly just to hear him laugh. I picked up Shaarac and swung him about. He was far too heavy for me to do so, but I still could for a moment, and it felt right. He giggled and out popped his Shaarvan dimples. It was a wonderful way to start the Tide. I joined in with my son's laughter.

We took the children to a nearby lake, rented a boat, and drifted about on the water. The inactivity of boating was not something either child apparently enjoyed. Shaarac wanted to swim, so Spelon rowed us to the edge of the lake, where piled sand made an ocean-like beach.

And then everyone's clothing came off except mine. I was still too shy for naked exposure. I sat on the sand and watched my sons playing in the water with Tevor and Thedar. That lasted a short time before I heard Spelon rip off his shirt then order me to don it.

I reared up at his tone but saw that he was only teasing me. I nodded, disrobed, slipped on the ridiculously oversized shirt, and jumped into the water. I suppose the seven or eight guards that were Tem's got an eye-full, but as Thal would have said, "Sometimes the penalty is worth the price."

Afterwards, when we were all dressed again, Spelon had to remain nude-chested. That was a nice bonus (for me.) As we walked back to our residence, several Shapechanger wives received rebukes from their lords for gazing at Spelon's magnificently muscled physique. Had we been anyone but Trendacons, I bet there might have been a bit of battle entanglement over Spelon's breach of Westlan attire, but we made it home without more than a few censuring looks from the women's husbands.

# *Chapter Seven*

## Tessa

This wasn't going to be easy, but then nothing worthwhile ever was. I chuckled to myself, knowing what to expect. They didn't disappoint me, those stuck in the status quo women. They'd all broken free from a system that dragged them through the mire, yet they were presently as stale as a fourTide leftover.

"We won't have her here," Merna said. "She's too young, too pretty, too tied to a male — to a bunch of males, and didn't you say there's a couple more of them in Altar?"

"Hunky, good-looking males, the ones we saw accompanying her," Frieda said, nodding her head as she licked her lips.

"Yeah, I wonder if she'll share?" Gertia said, looking at me to see if I'd approve of such a suggestion.

I'd assembled the Priestesses together, not to hear their complaints, but to inform them that Shaara would be joining them in a twoTide. They seemed not to understand the significance of my words.

"She is the Head's niece," I reminded them. "And an important player in Altar's future, and she may be the wife of our future leader. Maybe both. Do you realize what that means? Influence, heavy persuasion, a crack in the solidity of the Shapechanger world, and you're complaining that she's too pretty."

"And too young," Merna reminded me.

There were over twenty females in the Institute Hall, yet these three seemed to be the only ones speaking, or at least I thought so until Dora added her thoughts.

"She will tell the Shapechanger our secrets," she said. "Do we want that?"

"No!" all of them shouted out.

"On Altar, they have named her Queen," I said, hoping to jar the women into some semblance of future planning.

"That cannot be," Torrance said. "I am from Altar. I know it well. No female can gain authority. Women can't even speak on Altar. Female subjugation is in the laws."

Good, I thought. Something to fight, something to wake them up from their mind antiquity,

"The girl you wish to discard . . ." I began.

"Not discard, only allow to grow up," Merna said.

I ignored her and repeated. "The girl you wish to discard has already changed history. Altar has been in civil war for almost a threePass. Commoners vs Shapechanger. Those battles are now diminishing. The Shapechanger have beaten back the Commoners but at a big loss. All but one of the legislators in the Board of Elders are dead. The last one, Shaara's father, by the way, lies in a coma.

"Shaara's mother is now a member of the newly formed Board. The new government is being created with enhanced female rights. Many women fought in the war, holding weapons and battling beside husbands. Some fought, although their husbands were dead. Even perhaps some girls, those not spoken for, not created yet, were fierce combatants. You say Altar cannot change. It has.

"The fall of Altar rested on the shoulders of Shaara's brother. Except he did not admit to being her brother. He preferred to declare himself her husband. Then he proclaimed Shaara his heir and the Queen of all Altar. This King/Emperor died. Have Altarians rejected such a stance? Choosing to be governed by a woman? Not at all.

"The followers of Thenos have welcomed Shaara with open arms. She is more than a Queen to them. She is their liberator because Thenos painted pictures of her attributes — her loving nature, her kindnesses, the way she favored Commoners over Shapechanger, her beauty.

"The Commoners have never met Shaara, but they *know* her, or at least they believe they do". Thenos persuaded them with heavy doses of Power that still lingers and will probably always remain inside their belief system.

"And the baby Shaara birthed, although Thenos had never lain with her, was proclaimed to be his. Illogical but irrefutable in their minds, the baby you saw at the Testing is now the Prince of Altar. So, think of this when you urge me to cancel Shaara's Priestess rights. She will be raising the Crown Prince of Altar and is theoretically their Queen.

"But there is more to the girl than you comprehend. You saw her Power. She lit not just one candle but fifty. Then, when Merna complained about the expense of wasting so many, Shaara not only extinguished them but replaced them as new. For such an endeavor, she was called a show-off and overly proud, but you do not know her. She is neither. She is, in fact, unbelievably humble.

"But she needs our support, our training. Her temper flares, and she loses control. It is for that reason that we must offer her our patronage. She must learn to regulate her Power. So far, her temper has always been modified by intelligence. She is not a violent sort.

"I provoked her intentionally, and she retaliated as desired. Her revenge, her reprisal? She dumped a bucket of water over my head. No bucket was available. No water nearby. Yet, she acquired them. Which one of you has that kind of Power?

"Oh, there is one last item, before I dismiss you with the instruction that you must treat Shaara well when she enters into our midst a twoTide from now.

"You may have heard that the infamous Thenos has been killed. That is true, but the way it was done has been kept a secret. Hear me, my friends. Thenos met his Death at the hands of this girl that you wish to toss back into the Westlan pond of male dominance.

"Thenos discovered, to his amazement, that a Priestess, even an untrained one such as Shaara, can sever the currents that control the brain. Shaara had no need to bloody her hands or to call forth those huge, towering hunks of male muscles that surround her. In order to eradicate the problem that caused the downfall of the entire Altarian government, she did the deed herself. Alone.

"Afterwards, when Thenos lay mute before the Shapechanger, they stripped him of his military secrets. Then Shaara — sweet, demure, pretty, young Shaara, halted the tyrant's heartbeat. She killed the beast.

"So do not question her aptitude. Do not persist in denigrating her age, her appearance, or the males who accompany her. Shaara is one of us, and she will be welcomed as such."

I was through then. I'd said my full. Whether I'd convinced them or not did not matter. I was the head of the Institute and had the full backing of Westla.

Ignoring their questions and their stunned sputtering of past obstacles they'd like to strew into the air, and I strode off back to my house. Let them simmer through this Tide and into the next. What I'd needed to do was done.

If only such outpourings of truth resolved outdated issues of the status quo. I knew that Shaara would be a single flower amid a meadow of dead weeds. No wonder the Priestesses felt threatened.

If I cared for my position, if I were fully confident that Shaara wouldn't go back to being the footpad of a Shapechanger male, if I could clearly see the path of possibilities, perhaps I might fear her, too.

But then I remembered the sight of her just after she'd dumped water over my head — her gestures of contrition, her spouting of sorries, her bowed head, and the tears in her eyes. How could Shaara ever be someone to provoke alarm?

# Shaara

Thal always said that beginnings were a chance to discover *newness*. He was big on such things: a new flower, a species of tree uncategorized, an animal of a different type, an obstacle not yet surmounted. But he had always had more courage than I did.

The Tide had arrived when I must venture into the Priestess Institute, and I trembled. My stomach allowed no food to pass my lips for fear I'd vomit. My sleep-deprived brain felt hazy with stupidity.

If the women asked me to pass some test of entrance, I knew I would fail. On the whole, I was a quivering mess of nerves, and nothing my bondmates said to cheer me up could change those feelings.

My guardians walked me to the Institute in silence. Spelon had taken up his usual posture, his arm draped across my shoulder. He was not nervous about my entry into the Priestess Guild, but his ever-watchful attention still scanned the paths for danger. Tem's guards haunted our back, their pipes ready in case another Altarian wanted to capture me for the sake of their belief in my Queenship.

It was not a cheery way to journey to the Institute, but the only way we could. Shaarac was riding astride Thedar's massive shoulders. The child could see everything up there and thought it an exciting activity whenever a pseudo horse was available. With Tem's guards in attendance, my bondmates felt that the danger was less, so they could offer him this treat.

Tenor was carrying the baby. Thaandar was also awake. He was wide-eyed and interested in our walk. He was always a cheerful little boy unless he was hungry, which happened frequently. I suspected that meant that Thaandar would grow as big a Spelon. He had big feet, too.

I don't know what the males planned to do while I was inside learning Priestess secrets. The baby was bottle feeding, so it wasn't as difficult as it would have been if I were still nursing, but Thaandar was still in diapers. He would require bottles and changes while offering nothing more than his dimples and smiles.

Shaarac was a whirlwind, stirring up trouble, getting dirty, and exploring things he shouldn't. He would get cranky when he didn't get his way and fussy when he got tired. In other words, I was leaving my bondmates with a burdensome full-time job. It amazed me that they did so willingly and with great enthusiasm.

I thought about asking where they'd be, the subject a new thought to me, but Shapechanger preferred silence on the pathways so they could hear the approach of others. I would not risk anyone's safety in exchange for the relief of my curiosity.

We arrived at the Institute. Our silence continued. I guess they wondered what I would do next. I had no idea. Should I knock at the towering gate? Should I unfasten the gate lock and walk inside? Were males allowed entry? None of those questions had been answered because I'd never thought to ask.

But the huge gate to the building, one with elaborate scrolls and filigrees sketched in gold, magically opened, and three women stood in its portal. Only one held great Power. I recognized her from the Testing. Merna, I think, was her name. The others I'd never seen before.

"Only the Priestess may enter through this gate," Merna said in a grandiose and snotty manner.

I supposed that was to be expected. The Priestesses received homage all over Westla and probably other planets, as well. They were recognized as individuals with Privilege and Authority and were bowed to and sought out for problem-solving. Even male Shapechanger sometimes begged for their assistance in matters normally addressed only by other males. Priestesses were always offered the best of food, quarters, and servants wherever they went.

I turned to my guardians and sons and said my goodbye. I don't know why I was suddenly teary-eyed. Spelon wrapped me in his heavy arms and kissed me deeply. He was manifesting pure Shapechanger ownership, but I let it go. Changes were difficult, especially when they came from lifelong conditioning. The few slips that Spelon probably wasn't even aware of seemed easy enough to ignore. Besides, at that moment, I craved his attention. Changes were difficult for me, as well.

I walked inside with the females, heard the great door thunder closed behind us, and then listened to the cavernous stillness inside. The quiet suddenly ended. People would say silence offered no echoes, but for me, the impact was as great as the lash of a landoor's tail across my face. Centuries of women's voices began to whisper in my ears, tickle my belly button, and tug teasingly at my hair.

"I greet you all," I said, hoping to halt their overly enthusiastic salutations.

The two middle-aged Priestesses eyed me as if I'd been drinking crazy juice. "Who are you talking to?" one of them asked. "There's no one else here."

Merna said nothing. Her eyes took on a new aspect as if she were looking into my soul. I hoped not.

Ignoring whatever thoughts she'd had concerning my ghost greeting, she led us deeper into the building, only stopping when we reached a small doorway that showed a room with a couple of chairs, a table, a small cabinet, and a wall of purple cloth.

As I got closer, I realized that the cloth was actually different sizes of Priestess gowns hung from pegs in the wall. Merna glanced back at me, sized my frame then pulled down one of them. I could see that the gowns were all floor-length and long-sleeved without any trim or decoration.

Their deep purple color of a violet-amethyst hue shimmered slightly but not in a decorative way. I supposed my outfit didn't matter, but these were like gunny sacks, lacking any shape. No darts or diagonal cuts or gathered waist. The neckline had only the merest ribbon for comfort against skin chaffing. Honestly, they were completely boring.

I thought about how I used to design my own dresses using the ship's clothing machine, adding delicate piping or lace around the cuffs and neck. I'd sometimes added an overlay with contrasting fabric, something Shaarvan was not fond of, but had allowed while I was onboard the ship. I'd had fun with it, even in the days when a variety of colors hadn't been an option — until Shaarvan finally loosened up.

I think I sighed briefly, casting away such whimsy, but I shed my current dress and draped myself in the ugly Priestess uniform. The cotton-like socks I was given matched the dress fabric exactly. (One wouldn't want feet to acquire creativity.) The same color purple shoes were functionable but not something I'd ever wear outside the Institute. I mean, purple shoes? Really?

Next Merna ordered me to sit on a nearby chair, then picked up a pair of scissors, apparently ready to massacre my hair. I jumped up and whirled around.

"No," I said. "You will not cut my hair. That is an indisputable, definite NO."

The argument that proceeded lasted until the moment Tessa burst into the room. "What is all this yelling?" she demanded.

"Disobedience," Merna said. "Already, she displays not only her temper but her vanity. We cannot have this lack of discipline."

"I see," Tessa said. Her eyes surveyed my thick growth of hair. It had grown very long, falling down my back, probably all the way to my bottom.

"And your reason, Shaara?" she asked.

"Shaarvan ordered me never to cut it. Altarian women always have free flowing long hair. Don't they on Westla, as well?"

"The rules of the Institute state that a new Priestess must undergo hair cutting to demonstrate that she is leaving the old ways behind," Merna stated.

"Yes and to depart from the rules would force this whole institution to crumble, wouldn't it?" Tessa said sarcastically. "Give me the scissors, Merna. I will initiate Shaara."

Tessa took them in hand, reached over for a lock of hair, and snipped it before I could protest.

"There, the deed is done. Shaara, you can tell Shaarvan that you did not cut your hair but that I did. And no one else, but perhaps your males will notice the single lock I took."

Tessa set the scissors back on the table, handed the lock of hair to Merna, and then said, "What other tortures do you have planned for our newest novitiate?"

Merna ignored the remark about torture, but she was still not placated. "She cannot walk about like that. Everyone will see. They will know that you gave Shaara special privileges."

"I had my head sheared. It took a half-pass to grow it to its present length. This isn't fair," one of the two quiet ones said.

"What are your names?" I asked.

Tessa whirled around to stare at me. "You didn't get an introduction?" she said, obviously distressed by such a lack of manners.

"This is Grotha, and the other is Palla. You will be attending classes with them," Tessa told me.

"As to what you said, Grotha," Tessa lectured, "you will find that on Westla, genetics, Power, and ability hold weight. Fair for one is not fair for another. Shaara is a Trendacons. She will always get special privileges, and I told you already about her abilities. I suggest that instead of complaining about how things are, you work on improving your *own* Power."

I was not starting off on the right foot, as they used to say in my home world. I didn't know if Westla had a similar expression, but the truth was that with Tessa's censure, I was positive I was making enemies, not the friends I'd hoped for.

Perhaps Tessa read the thought. The corner of her eyes crinkled with good humor. "Thal told me your thoughts often made him smile. You are good at that, my dear. Let us see if we can move forward on the right foot now," she said with a cackle.

We must have made a strange parade, our identical deep purple gowns swaying as we walked. I reached up and twisted my hair about, then braided it tightly. I hadn't done so in a long time, but remembering what Grotha had said, I thought it might be more politically correct than leaving my hair long and flowing.

Tessa noticed my fingers weaving the strands together and cracked a wry smile, then nodded that braiding my hair was an appropriate move to make. When I tucked the braid under, like I'd done on Freinana sometimes, Tessa grinned even wider.

The Institute had classrooms, not unsimilar to a high school, except with fewer rooms. But novitiates, which is what I was told I was called, were obviously placed in their levels. As to whether that was based on ability or time spent at the Institute, I wasn't informed.

Our teacher was named Chasta, which sounded too similar to chastity, but I held my smile just in case someone besides Tessa was proficient at mind reading, and I carefully controlled my projections. That was still a challenge for me, but I was learning.

I settled into the seat I was assigned, then wondered if I was supposed to be taking notes, but no one seemed to have paper or pencils. Palla and Grotha had both taken seats at the rear, although there were still empty seats beside me. Had the young neophytes chosen that distance, or were all seats assigned?

Merna evidently had completed her task. She left, but Tessa sat down in the corner as if she'd decided to stay and observe.

I don't think Chasta liked Tessa's being there, but she pretended not to notice. She also ignored me most of the time. The lesson pertained to, whoops, I wasn't allowed to mention such things outside the Institution. I wondered for the first time what I would tell my guardians at the end of the Tide.

*You will tell them nothing, just like with your lessons at my house,* Tessa's thought popped into my head. It jarred me enough to break my concentration so that I dropped the book I was supposed to be . . . whoops.

I received no scolding for my lack of concentration. Others were dropping things as well. In fact, if anything, my collapse seemed to make the teacher less standoffish. She almost smiled until she remembered that I was apparently on her *I don't like your list.*

Such was my first Tide and the many that followed. Tessa often stayed nearby, which was a good thing since negative vibes were abundant, and her presence seemed to offer a buffer to some extent.

But I was willing to endure such things as long as I was learning, and although many of the lessons were too easy for me, I was practicing concepts I'd never learned before, as well as developing ways around the constant disapproval of both teachers and fellow apprentices.

Attendance was a fourTide sequence followed by a twoTide break. Tem insisted on meeting with me sometimes. He claimed it was because he was my uncle and wanted to socialize, but I think he was checking on my progress, making sure I wasn't becoming Power-aggressive.

The dinners included Tessa, Shaarac, and the baby, plus my guardians, and while eating delicious entrees we were able to pepper Tem with questions about the latest news from Altar. That was the good part, although the news was always sparse.

On our second dinner with him, Tem brought up Thal's send-a-way. I felt guilty that I'd hadn't thought about Thal's funeral in a twentyTide. Thal's body had been processed long ago, dehydrated, and capsulated into a baby-sized, bullet-shaped object, but I'd asked if we could send him to a star, and we still hadn't done that.

My bondmates and I decided that the following Tide would be good for his final send-off. Thal's family had long ago passed on, and we were all he had left, so there was no one to consult for approval or scheduling.

The capsule was delivered to us the next morning. Both Tessa and Tem walked with us to the Space Port, but they went no further. I had asked to carry Thal, and I did so for a while, but the capsule contained a firing mechanism as well as his dried remains and was far heavier than it looked. Spelon passed the baby to Tenor, Shaarac rode on Thedar's shoulders, and Spelon carried Thal the rest of the way.

It didn't really matter where we released the death capsule. It was already programmed for its destination, but we had decided to head for Thal's ship. That seemed the best place for our remembrance ceremony. When we reached our location, we each said a few words about our favorite memory. I thanked Thal for Thaandar and for his guidance through many Passes.

Shaarac understood that we were saying our last goodbye. When it was his turn to speak, he said, "Bye bye, Daddy," but seemed to accept that Thal, at least the Thal he remembered, was not really in the capsule. After that, we did not linger long.

Thedar switched on the program, and the Death capsule soared upward toward the Great Saberey Eye. I had a moment of worry that the gate would not sense its approach and the capsule might crash into it, but the Great Saberey Eye opened wide, and Thal shot upward and out into space.

We watched until the Eye slowly closed again, then treaded back to West. We were not required to pass through the decontamination chambers, so our way was cut in half, but even so, Tessa and Tem had not remained. We had not really expected them to stay, however. As Thedar said, we still needed to return home and process Thal's departure.

The males drank to their grief if that's what they were feeling. I played with the children. Both boys were quiet, tired out from the trek, and were soon put to bed. So, whatever mourning process I was supposed to do was pretty much done on my own. I fled to the bedroom, stripped down, and crawled into bed. That seemed the best use of free time. Sleep welcomed me.

# *Chapter Eight*

## Shaara

Of course, I knew that Tessa wouldn't be staying near me forever inside the Institute. I guessed one Tide she'd disappear, and I'd be facing teachers and learners on my own. But even so, it was a surprise when that Tide arrived. Chasta's class was the first. I noticed right off that the chair where Tess usually sat was absent. That should have alerted me, but it didn't. I was halfway through class when I felt the teacher's increase of antagonism.

"No, not that way, Shaara. How incompetent. Have you learned nothing?"

I had learned a great deal, but confronting a teacher in front of her students was not something I chose to do. I buckled down and concentrated harder, but everything I tried to do seemed to go wrong. I dropped, misplaced, picked incorrectly, got elbowed, tripped, and kneed. It was not a good Tide.

When the next Tide passed in the same manner, I began to doubt myself. But then my senses started buzzing from interference, and I realized that I was being magically influenced to fail. The faint smell of burned bread I breathed in reinforced that idea. I'd smelled it often at Tessa's house since she relied on magic for many of her exploits. But this magic wasn't hers. I would have recognized her essence.

After that, as I journeyed from class to class, I picked up the scent of gasoline, envy's announcement. It lingered in certain areas surrounding various teachers. A haze of yellow, although faint, informed me that anger also rode in the currents of air. The anger of experienced Priestesses, not students like Grotha and Palla. I was being targeted.

I had personally found that anger is often a bad emotion to allow free rein, but it was also a resource for pooled Power. Like a swimming pool used by firemen to put out a fire, it stood ready for use.

As my own anger brewed higher, I cornered it and prepared it for manipulation. I would not release vengeance on students who were simply following the air strands of whispered instruction. I would strike at the instigators. I wished I could talk with Tessa about the situation, but she was absent, and I was alone amidst a sea of magical vipers.

In the last class of the Tide, I encountered another obstacle course of disablements. Like the cobwebs of an early morning's walk, I brushed them aside, sending their senders into whirling dervishes. The more horrific the sending, the faster their spin. Students gaped at their teachers. They had no idea what was causing the mass craziness. Like them, I sat Google-eyed in wonder at how well it had worked.

Palla, who'd often exchanged a faint smile with me, exchanged seats to sit closer. "What is going on?" she asked me,

I shrugged, wanting no part in claiming this spectacle.

It was at that moment that Tessa walked into the room where we were sitting. She crooked her finger and beckoned me out of the room. Again, I shrugged, smiled back at Palla, and followed Tessa.

"What did they do to you?" Tessa asked when she had me in a quiet corner.

"It would be easier if you read my thoughts," I said, neither denying nor admitting the deed.

It only took a moment for Tessa to see the two Tides of negative magic. She scanned them thoroughly and then asked for permission to view them a second time.

"I see," she said when she'd processed it. "Can you stop the spinning?"

I nodded, waiting to see what punishment Tessa would render, but I was already fed up with the Institute enough to call it quits. Whatever she and Tem needed to do . . .

"Please stop, Shaara."

Tessa had never used please with me before, not that I could remember. But I would ponder that another time. I closed my eyes, pulled back the swimming pool of Power, and stopped the whirling dervishes. Most of the teachers collapsed in place, sinking to the ground from exhaustion. I knew that only because I felt the cessation and the depletion of their energies. Had I also robbed them of their Power?

Another question for later. First, I must pay the penalty, whatever Tessa designated, but her reprimand would also determine my willingness to return to the Institute. Perhaps Westla was not the right place for me to be. Would it be safe to return to Deathstar or the other planet with the fierce predators we'd live on? Or was it time to journey to Altar and . . ."

"There will be no punishment for you, Shaara," Tessa said. "You have handled yourself, under great duress, most appropriately. It is the others who will be punished. But please do not leave for Altar or the other places you're considering. The time is not right. I cannot see your path yet, but there will be one, and then we will make a decision."

She was smiling at me with kindness in her eyes. Tessa, kind? But then she had always helped me. I guess she'd become my friend. I just never realized it.

I inhaled a deep breath of air, then admitted my guilt. "But I took revenge, Tessa. Tem will not like that. He warned me to always guard my temper."

"And you did, Shaara. Like the bucket of water, your retaliation was not deadly. You moderated your attack. I am proud of you for your control. Call your bondmates, and you are free to leave."

"Permanently?"

She stared into my eyes a moment, searching. "Are you learning anything here? Will attendance assist you with your Power?"

"If the situation were different. . ."

Tessa also took in a large intake of air. I could tell that she'd identified the odors in the air as I had: jealousy, envy, dislike, anger.

"They were foolish. None of them have any idea what you are capable of," she said, heaving a vast sigh of sadness.

"Shaara, you are my heir. When my time comes, it will be you in charge of the Institute. Tem knows that."

I was shaking my head. "That's not what I want."

"I know," she said. "There are crossroads. Shaarvan has made no choice in his future either. Perhaps you will remain on Altar. Perhaps you will return here. I cannot foresee. There will be many options, but whatever the decisions you make, classes here will be open to you *if* you can face the fools and the foolish.

"Unfortunately, the unwise are everywhere, Except for the unpopulated planets you were thinking about, but would someplace like that be best for your sons and for the guardians who have pledged their lives to you?"

I didn't respond. I was thinking about that. I'd never realized how much I held the reins of our family's future. I'd always thought it was Shaarvan who controlled our lives.

"Come, I sense your bondmates' approach. We must meet them at the gate, or they might be tempted to tear it asunder."

"But what will I tell them?" I worried.

"I shall handle it."

# Thedar

I suspected immediately that something had happened at that Priestess school. We'd all felt a great rush of suffering, Shaara's projections hitting us from the park where we entertained the children. As one, we collected the boys and headed back to the Institute at a fast pace, feeling the urgent need to comfort her and surround her with our love.

Tessa met us at the gate and explained simply that Shaara was tired and needed a few Tides of rest. Fine with us. We did not care if she ever returned, but the moodiness in Shaara's posture and face told us that there was more to it than that.

Shaara had been hurt — not physically. They would not dare. But something had buffeted our girl in a way we could not defend against. My anger boiled. I clenched both teeth and fists.

I wanted to drag more information from Tessa, but she had closed off from us. Priestess secrets, I assumed. The expression and words of Tessa told us that we were not allowed to know the details. I growled at the same moment Spelon did. We exchanged looks and nodded in agreement.

Tessa scanned us. *Leave it,* she spoke into my mind. *The child dealt with it. She will be fine.*

I nodded that I had received her message. I did not know if Tessa had said the same to all three of us or just to me, but that did not matter. What mattered is that we had sent a happy woman into the Institute and were getting one back who was if not miserable, close enough to it. And it had not just been this Tide, but increasingly each time we collected her.

I made the decision at that moment that Shaara needed trees. Although she said she was too tired, we all insisted on a trip to the forest. When Thedar mentioned *giant* trees, Shaarac was sold. He started his *pleases* with his Shaarvan dimples on full display. Shaara could never resist that.

We had all learned long ago that with Shaara, trees were restorative. We had witnessed that on Deathstar and on our stay on the moon of some unknown planet that Thal never named. The scent of pine, the texture of bark, the calm atmosphere was all she needed when she was hurt by happenstance, a sour word, or when missing Shaarvan brought her low.

When we arrived in the center of a huge grove of dark wood pine, Shaara sat down on the barky compost as if it were the softest padded seat. She was still in her dark purple Priestess gown, but she did not seem to care if it picked up dirt or tore from the roughness of the forest's bark shavings spread across the ground.

Spelon wanted her to move to a nearby fallen tree, a far friendlier place to sit, but Shaara shook her head, only barely holding back her tears. It seemed that she needed total immersion in the element because she lay down in the middle of the roughness and let out a huge sigh. I wondered if a Shapechange would lighten her mood and suggested it, but the children were not able to change yet, and Shaara rejected the idea.

The forest was silent. No others were hiking that Tide. Whatever animals resided there kept away from us, possibly noting our nature, but then all of Westla were Shapechanger.

Shaara had often told of us about birds that chirped and tweeted in the trees and the sky of her home world, but the forests of Westla had few birds. I wished for her sake that we could introduce their noisy banter just to cheer her up. Would flying things light up her eyes as well as trees did?

Shaara had once told us of a bird bluer than lake water with a top-notch of cobalt feathers that stood upright in a crest. She said the bluejay was louder than all the other birds, scolding them and bossing them around, which, the way Shaara told it, was a good thing because he was the most beautiful of all birds.

I wondered, at the time, if her tale of a bluejay was possible or just some fiction she had made up. But as new as Shaara was then, she could not have told a false story. And I had believed that maybe her imagery was describing Shaarvan. Except Shaarvan would never wear blue, which was the color favored by Commoners.

Whether the tale was true or fiction, I wished for a bluejay to taunt Shaara with its scolding, teasing her back into smiles.

Shaara was lying on the ground with her limbs spread out, her braided hair picking up twigs and pieces of bark. Spelon sat down beside her and asked if she wanted her hair loosened. She nodded, so he untwined it and let it go free. The braid had left ripples across her free-flowing hair. Spelon set to work untangling the knots and removing tiny bits of forest. I watched as Shaara sat up and leaned back into him, relaxing.

In another tale of her home world, Shaara told us of an apparatus that took pictures. If I had one, I would have used it at that moment. Shaara was always pleasing to look at, but at that moment, she was perfection. Her hair was strewn out as if she were just waking from a night's sleep. Her face had relaxed as if all the cares of the world had dropped away, and the faint smile of serenity as Spelon worked his magic on her scalp and hair made it a picture worth remembering.

Camera, that's what she had called it. A camera. A recording device of memories. What a brilliant idea. If only Thal were here to invent one for us.

I stood up and moved away, checking to see what Tenor was up to. He had both children with him. Shaarac was finding pine cones. He'd accumulated quite a pile. The baby was sleeping in Tenor's lap. Tenor also needed his picture taken. He looked like a Shapechanger who had found his contentment.

# *Chapter Nine*

## Tem

A dark yellow haze lies heavy around me, and rotting pampa fruit exudes its stench throughout the hall. If any of the Priestesses doubt my anger, they have only to see its signs and smell its odor. I am a raging Saberey whose patches darken along my jawline and across my nose. Probably small black dots are vivid beneath the spiny whiskers that poke through my visage.

I want to rend their bodies with my terrible fury. If they are not adroit in their apologies, it will be done. I allow Priestesses to inhabit West. It is a complementary component when handled well, but they have betrayed the Trendacons, and my patience is at an end.

I have looked the other way too many times. Tessa is one of the deserving ones. She carries her load and does it well. She is loyal to West and to Westla. I have no quarrel with her. But the other women . . .

They are filtering in. Their dark purple gowns hide the ugliness inside them. I don't restrain the roar that comes rushing out of my mouth. I want them to feel my anger, to let them know that their lives are in jeopardy.

Taking note of my angry roar, several turn, heading back to the entrance. My soldiers repel them. There will be no exit until I have lashed my irritation in their faces. They have forgotten their position. They think they are equal, but they are not. My troops are fewer now.

Many are in Altar, but I have enough to slay every single Priestess if needs be.

I roar once more. It feels good. I thought about completing my change, letting out the Saberey, but then I could not tell them my thoughts on their actions. They must hear words, not the snarls of an angry beast.

Tessa moves to stand beside me. She and I are close. We have dined often together. We often meet each other's needs. We are one in this. Her anger threatens to boil over in a different shape. She is thinking about scalding them with boiling water, freezing off their lips, and sprinkling sores onto the bottom of their feet. I smile at her, liking her thoughts. Perhaps her ideas are only to calm me down, but the heat of her rage is equally fierce. We are both enflamed.

The women huddle together in the center of the hall. Tessa nods that they are all present, all except the neophytes. Tessa told me that Shaara said they were not involved. I have doubts about that, but I accept what Tessa gleaned from Shaara. The child might not have shown her everything, but Tessa said the child was too crushed to hide much.

Tessa begins, relating what had been done to our girl. Several bite their lips, look down, pretend humbleness. I can read them; every thought is a banner that flies through my mind, identifying, organizing, and displaying until I have labeled each guilty party as well as the ring leader of the harassment.

The haze of yellow sinks lower, encompassing the group completely. Do they know what it signifies? Do they understand that I am judging their crimes?

Tessa tells them what Shaara did as revenge. Surprise wreathes their faces. They hadn't associated their wild spinning dervishes with the young woman they bullied and browbeat.

But as Tessa continues, the ringleader speaks. She is called Merna. I recall her from the testing, stating that Shaara should not be accepted because she was too young, too pretty, too incapable of withstanding the stress of training.

"There. I told you so. She is unsuitable for the Institute. Already, she cracked under the stress and sent her untrained magic into our midst."

I let out another roar, this one louder than the last. Too bad Merna is such a bony old witch. There is no good eating in a body that is parched with vileness.

"I believed that you were smarter than you are, Merna," Tessa says, her voice sounding calm while the lava inside her rises.

"Hump, if you listened to me more, you'd find out that I'm a lot smarter than you think."

"I see. Did it occur to you that Shaara sent a web that ensnared every one of you who tormented her? And she instructed her magic to make the worst of those offenders whirl faster and harder than the others. Pretty clever for an untrained Priestess. I wonder if she even debated delivering harsher punishments. She is capable of such, as you remember from my tale about Thenos."

"Yes," Merna says, tossing her head as if she is not only proud of what she had led the others to do but believing that her attack on Shaara gives her power towards becoming a leader, possibly even replacing Tessa,

What vanity. What a fool. As if I would allow *her* to take over the Institute.

Assuming we are captivated by her treachery, she continues. "As I said before, Shaara is too dangerous to have around. You must ship her off the planet."

I yowl at that, but I do not roar. I am too intrigued by what Tessa will say and do in response."

"Would that be a sufficient punishment for Merna?" Tessa asks softly.

Merna glances at her fellow Priestesses, but no one is backing her. In fact, they shift away, already seeing where this is going.

"She was informed that Shaara was a Trendacons, right?" I ask, already knowing the answer to that.

Tessa nods and says, "Yes."

"Then she deserves the full punishment. Death descends on all who harm a Trendacons."

"But Shaara is only a girl, one who has lost her husband due to her meddling in Priesthood magic. Surely, you can't defend her in this."

"She is my niece. Her two children are my nephew's sons. She has been accepted into the family in all ways. And she is *Saberey*."

Merna is looking all around for someone to be on her side. Her quick search is not successful. "Forgive me, Lord, Head of Westla. I did not know her lineage."

An immediate odor of sulfur permeates the room. Merna should be buckling over from the lie, discarding her stomach contents on the ground, but she is apparently not Shapechanger enough to feel the lie — for a moment. Then she retches onto the ground and spits out the truth. "I did know Shaara's lineage."

"Why did you torment her?" I ask, hardly caring at that point. The woman disgusts me, and I have no more patience for her lies and excuses.

"She threatens my future, my lord. I was jealous."

Few people know that the great hall is a window into the Saberey forest. The walls are porous for them. At that moment, the walls darken, and the foggy haze grows more prominent. Then, shadows of the Saberey become visible.

The cats of my family often peek in to see what is occurring on Westla, but it is unexpected for them to appear in matters unrelated to grave issues of state. Shaarvan had said the pack accepted Shaara into their midst. Perhaps they deem this situation important.

Rarely do the Saberey show themselves even this much, but as we watch, their faces turn clearer until I can name each of them present. The great She-Cat, leader of the group, nods to me, then lets out a rumble at Merna. With tigers,, that is far more significant than my angry roar, but I have found that most Shapechanger do not know the tones of tigers and respect the loudness of my roar more than the simple rumble.

Merna obviously does not know this fact either. She stares at them, giving no honor to their presence in the hall. She eyes them as if they are a mere hindrance, taking up her time.

"We have been with Shaarvan," the great one says to me. "We are not pleased with his actions and told him so with our claws." She arches them. One could call it showing off the sharpness — if one dared.

"Now we have listened to this poor excuse for a Priestess. She attacked our Shaara, blood of our blood. Let no one henceforth treat our offspring so dishonorably. You are warned, Priestesses. Shaara is special and favored. She is ours.

"*Batner*, take this unworthy one, this disgrace to the honor of all Shapechanger. We shall hunt tonight, not for good eating, but for the sport."

An image from the wall disconnects itself, leaps down on the ground, opens its huge mouth, and grabs Merna's head, then as quickly jumps back into the wall, carrying her with him. The action has lasted only an instant, not even long enough for Merna to issue a scream.

A stunned group of women watches as all the Saberey fade.

The Priestesses turn with gaping mouths to regard me.

"Is she dead?"

"Will they bring her back?"

"Are we in jeopardy, too?"

The last question seems to provoke an even bigger silence as they all wait for me to speak.

"Is there anyone here who plans further harm to my niece?"

A flurry of headshaking meets my question.

"Have you learned what befalls any who mistreatment Shaara?"

The nods of the women are emphatic. No one seems eager to disagree.

"Guards, open the door. The Priestesses are leaving."

The rush out would have been a stampede if there were more Priestesses, but they all cram themselves through the door and bolt away, probably running the entire distance back to the Institute.

"That covers it perfectly," I say, grinning at Tessa.

She cackles wildly, thrilled with the punishment of Merna, who had so often been a disruptive irritant.

"Now, do you think you can get our girl to return to the Institute?" I ask.

Tessa nods, looking thoughtful. "Yes, she has fortitude, and she wants to please your nephew. Shaarvan ordered her to train. So, yes."

"Interesting dialog with the She-Cat."

"I agree. Shaarvan is getting bombarded on all fronts. I imagine Tren is doing his job to try and persuade Shaarvan, too. And Teea will also be demanding her daughter back. Any word on Tevor?"

I shake my head. I wish I had more information on his well-being. My brother had been gravely injured by Thenos, who had administered deadly drugs to all the Elders of Altar. The fact that Tevor is the only one still alive is a wonder. The thought of his departure from this realm causes me much pain.

"Quite a showing from the Saberey," Tessa says, staring at the now-empty walls. "So unexpected."

I nod as we walk out of the Great Hall together. The last time the Saberey showed themselves like that had been at the acceptance of my role as head of Westla. It had been a great honor. And now they show their esteem for Shaara. That was interesting. The girl continues to amaze me.

I had plans to spend the evening with Temina. I did so weekly. Sometimes, she welcomed me. Other times, she ignored me. I never knew what to expect, yet still, I knew I owed her my time. She was my wife, after all. I had done this to her, caused her mind to depart from reality.

A night with Tessa would be sweeter, but she knew my schedule, so we parted amiably and went our separate ways.

# Shaara

My mates took me to a landoor ranch. I couldn't believe it. Why hadn't I been told before that there were landoors on Westla? Tenor had discovered the ranch on the Westlan equivalent of the Yellow Pages. (That was somewhat like a telephone book, a pre-Internet invention.)

When I saw the landoors, I squealed most indecorously. Shaarvan would have punished me for such a breach, but the males simply laughed and praised Tenor for his success at finding my happiness.

The landoors were for hire. I walked through their midst, rosy with joy. The owner looked worried. "They are tame, my lady," he said, "but if you are not familiar with the species, they might injure you. Their hooves are heavy. When they step on you, it hurts."

"I know. I am more than familiar with them. I worked on a ranch in Freinana. I rode all the owner's landoors. Which one has the best paces, the most spirit?"

The owner, Toron, bowed in deference, especially when Tenor mentioned our family name was Trendacons, but he was still not persuaded to open his stables to my full inspection. Instead he turned to Tenor, who seemed to be in charge of our group that excursion, viewed with awe Spelon's chest of muscles, then scanned the boys and Thedar.

"Surely, you will not wish this young mistress to walk among the landoor and claim one of her choice? I can recommend a gentle mare she could sit on."

Spelon snorted. "She is a Priestess, not a young mistress. She is the niece of the Head One, Tem. I would not doubt her word about her skills with landoors if I were you."

Toron turned his eyes to me then. The pupils widened. He did not dare disbelieve Spelon, but he seemed to want to. "Is she not too young for the Priesshood? They are always old crones. Surely, you jest. Which of you lords owns her?"

That was enough of that. I pulled my eyes away from inspecting the landoor, flashed green eyes, and inserted my mind into the almost Powerless Shapechanger. "Bring your best landoor, a show quality gelding, saddled and ready for riding. No further admonishments or inquisitiveness into our business," I commanded.

The male's sputter was satisfying, but he didn't stick around long enough for me to savor (or feel guilty) for my brief excursion into Shapechanger Mind control.

"Shame on you," Thedar said lightly, but his eyes held more pride in my ability than scolding over the act.

Tenor did admonish me. "Well done, but do not do it again. You know better than that, especially with a Shapechanger male."

"He will talk of this. That is not wise, little one," Thedar added.

I shrugged. "I am thinking about leaving wisdom behind. It has gotten boring."

Spelon chuckled, which my two older bondmates didn't like. They turned solemn expressions in his direction, scarcely a moment away from rebuking him, but then Toron returned, leading a fine bay gelding: his coat shiny with good health, his legs a piece of poetry, his noble head nicely arched, and his eyes deep with intelligence. Perfect.

I stepped forward slowly, my hand out, although I had no carrot to feed him. He touched me with his muzzle, sniffed, then nickered softly. Recognition stirred our senses. He was a sensitive, that rare beast that could meet a Shapechanger's mind. Although on Freinana the landoors had been skittish around Shapechanger, this steed was obviously used to us. He felt no fear, only mild curiosity as he eyed the males. One hoof pawed at the ground, displaying his willingness to be ridden.

"I fear he will be too much for you, my lady," Toron said, having second thoughts about bringing this particular animal.

I ignored his words. "What is his name?" I asked.

A typical question for landoor ignorants. Names were nothing to the landoor. They did not view one as a mark of identification. It was a bipedal institution with no value.

Toron did not dare smirk at the question, however. He said, "I call him Mandar."

It was a Freinanan word meaning *handsome*. Not a bad name, and I supposed it fit, but I might rename him. On Freinana, I had given each one of the landoors their own special name. They seemed to respond to it.

I reached up and petted Mandar's great head. He lowered it into my hand, liking my touch, wanting more of it. I scratched around his ears. Not a favorite. I tickled under his chin. Still not his choice. Ah, near his right eye. That was the key to Mandar. He pushed against my hand and almost purred.

I took his head in my hand and lightly blew into his nostrils. For a moment, we shared breath, forming a relationship. Mandar approved. He pawed again, requesting further attention.

"Yes," I said as I walked to the saddle's stirrup. I checked the girth. Still tight. Toron had not tested my knowledge, probably too afraid of a mishap. Mandar was tall. I requested a hand-up. Toron attended to that, but he was about to lecture me on my unworthiness or some such bunk. I shook my head at him. His words died.

I swung my leg over, landed softly, and adjusted to the feel of Mandar. Toron was holding the bridle, still doubtful for my safety.

"Let go," I ordered.

He turned to my mates, asking permission. Fool. I had shown him more than he deserved, and he still had qualms about who I was. Seeing something in Tenor's eyes, Toron wisely relinquished his hold. I gave Mandar the slightest shift, allowing him to walk forward. He set off with a saucy prance.

"Direct me to the arena," I said.

Our group moved forward as one. I glanced down at Shaarac and thought a moment. Do you have any small landoors, miniatures for children?"

Toron shook his head nervously. "I have an old landoor, as gentle as a chair. He will permit a sitting child and not move an inch."

"Shaarac?" Would you like to try riding?"

Mandar was side-stepping a bit, tired of the conversation. He wanted a good gallop. I could feel that in him. I understood the feeling.

Shaarac did not seem eager in his response. He didn't want to look a coward, but a landoor was a giant next to him. He was probably wishing he could suck his thumb, but he restrained himself. He was too old for such things; he'd tell us now and then as if we were asking.

"I want to watch you, Mommy."

Mommy. I hadn't heard that in a while. Shaarac thought it babyish and had weaned himself to Mom.

"And you guys?" Anyone else want to saddle up?"

None of them looked enthusiastic. Thedar answered for them. "Like Shaarac, we prefer to watch you enjoy yourself."

Having done my duty to my companions, I allowed Mandar to step forward, and we entered the fenced-in area. His prancing increased. He had springs in his pace. I relished it.

"Trot," I said, not knowing whether he'd been worked on a long-line and knew his oral directives. Either my seat position or the word signified his advance in speed. He was willing.

His trot was too tense to be comfortable. He needed a gallop to refine it, but he also needed to feel my guidance to develop trust in my control. I worked him in several circles, then allowed a slow canter. Once more, the choppiness of his gate was a bit jarring.

I wondered how long it had been since he'd been run. Was he allowed the freedom of the ring? Or a long line to relieve his kinks? I would do both next time. Still, I continued as if training him. We both needed the exercise the sharing of team work.

I sat back, pulling him back into a trot. He didn't like that. He wanted to proceed into a gallop, but he was a gentleman. A single head toss communicated his dislike for the slower pace, but he buckled down, his head arching into the bit, our flow more even, more restrained.

"Ok, boy. You have earned a little freedom," I said, and I gave him the command. His head tucked, not from rebellion, but from his eagerness to run. I was ready for it. He was close to a good hard buck, but I didn't allow it. He let out a swift hind kick and a roll of the head. I pulled him back down and soothed his soul.

We continued the workout for a rather long time. I forgot the others, lost in the joy of riding. Mandar got his gallop and a full selection of his paces. He was untrained in dressage. He didn't know anything about leg pressure. He would need a lot of work. I would be happy to supply that.

I cooled him down and headed for the gate. Mandar was relaxed and content. He knew it was time for his stall and a good feed. He deserved it.

I handed him back to Toron, ignoring the man's over abundance of praise and his babbles of admiration for my riding skills. I was strangely fatigued; all those unused muscles complained of my long time in the saddle. Spelon gave support to my body. I leaned into him.

"Overdo it a bit?" he asked, and I looked up at him and smiled.

"Yes, but it was so worth it."

I wanted to buy Mandar, move to the ranch, and immerse myself back in the world of landoors, but I knew that wasn't possible. My guardians had already wasted half a Tide on my compulsion. It wasn't fair to them. At least Shaarac hadn't been bored. He'd found a small podo, a dog-like creature that loved retrieving thrown sticks, especially by someone whose toss wasn't very far. The two were having a great time.

"Shaarac, we go now," Thedar ordered. Without complaint, Shaarac came running towards us.

"You ride good, Mom," my son said, his eyes wide with admiration. "Maybe I ride, too, next time?"

"Did you pay Toron?" I asked Tenor since this whole event had been by his arrangement.

Westla didn't use coins exactly. I really didn't understand how payments were made. It was another area of living here I needed to investigate, but since Tenor had taken care of it, I let the matter drop. I was too tired to even think.

We had walked to the ranch, a long distance. I needed to rest before we headed back, but I hated to seem weak. "Could we sit down a few minutes until I get my breath back?" I asked.

"You were sitting," Shaarac said quite logically.

We asked and discovered that the ranch had an outdoor seating arrangement with a cover, cold drinks, and snacks. All of that was welcome. It restored me somewhat, but I still dreaded the long walk home.

Thedar had given Thaandar a bottle while we sat, so of course, the baby did what all babies do and discarded a previous meal into his diapers. It was my turn to change him, but Thedar wouldn't allow me to do so. "Rest," he said. "The necessary room has a cleaner."

Toron had hooked up Mandar to a cool-down machine. He was just returning the animal to its stall when we passed by. "Come back any time," the Shapechanger said.

I patted Mandar and said my goodbyes, thanking Toron for letting me ride his prize landoor. I think that amused him, but he'd already parceled out an adequate supply of compliments for my handling of the landoor. He may have worried that he'd offended one of my guardians. He said nothing more, just did a head bow and led Mandar back into the stable.

Shaarac gave out before we reached the end of the long path away from the ranch. Tenor picked him up and settled him around his shoulders, Shaarac's favorite post. Thaandar, contentedly full and ready for a nap, was already sleeping in Thedar's arms. I looked at my sons with a bit of envy, wishing I could rest in strong Shapechanger arms. I suppose my thought drifted into Spelon's head because, without a word, he hoisted me up in his arms and began carrying me.

"You don't have to do that," I said. "I'm not . . ."

"I know," he said. "But it is nice to be able to hold you. I think you are finally too exhausted to be prickly about it."

# *Chapter Ten*

## Tessa

At one point, I would have scorned Shaara's connection with her guardians. Who knew that such a relationship could resolve into a positive need-fulfilling symbiosis? The males no longer shoveled out commands or insisted that Shaara act in a certain manner. They took care of the boys and pretty much supplied her with all her needs for companionship and sex — at least the brawny, muscled guy did. It was most impressive the way the four-way bond had transformed.

It made me wonder if such a connection were possible on a wider range, but then there was no question that Shaara was unique. What she could orchestrate in her pseudo-family might not apply to anyone else.

The bondmates had certainly taken a depressed young woman and pumped her full of endorphins, the happy juice my old friend Thal used to talk about. Shaara had been re-vitalized almost magically. I wondered about the bondmates' secret, but I had no time for such tangents. I needed to get Shaara back into the Institute before Tem's traumatic assembly faded into memory. As if Saberey suddenly coming alive from wall images could ever be forgotten.

I wondered if there had been nightmares roaming the sleeping rooms of the Institute. If so, the women deserved them. Even if Shaara hadn't been a Trendacons, that treatment of any neophyte needed to be abolished. No slightly younger or prettier Priestess should ever be made to suffer the jealousy of the older hags.

Additionally, I feared that Shaara would have lost interest in perfecting her abilities. Her eagerness had certainly been mashed into stale pampa juice. I hoped that I could talk her back into her former enthusiasm.

I had come at the time of their morning eating cycle. I begged for a cup of *Cha,* and Thedar brought it to me. I slipped into a spare chair, his, I think, and asked about their activities for the past twoTide. As suspected, they had taken Shaara to a nearby forest. Shaarvan had once spoken of the girl's affinity for trees, not uncommon for the Trendacons who often categorized such as sacred.

But I was surprised to hear of a landoor ranch. For one thing, I only vaguely remembered hearing about Shapechanger, who insisted on resurrecting whatever familiarity they carried with them from their home worlds. Landoors, that was something new. A faint tickle of a memory hinted that Freinana, the planet where Shaara had been taken after her kidnapping, might have been the origin of such an animal. Had Tem told me that?

But discussing an obscure animal was not the purpose of my visit. I needed to wrestle the Institute into our conversation. I needn't have worried about it. Shaara tossed it into the ring without a pause.

"You've come to take me back," she said.

"Yes. You need the instruction. But . . ."

"Okay," she said, as easily as that.

"Good."

"We need to discuss this," Spelon said.

Shaara placed her hand on his beefy arm. I wondered how that felt. Not to be like Gertia, who seemed sex-starved in spite of the abundance of Shapechanger males always willing to perform, but I noted in myself a brief quiver of desire to test this one's mettle myself. Of course, I would never act on it.

Tem and I were not exclusive, but irrational itches were not a wise course of action. My eyes traveled to the other two. Worthy specimens, but I decided that it would be better not to violate Shaara's web of guardians. Her closeness with me was too important.

Meanwhile, as hormones were playing tricks on an old woman, I overheard Shaara soothing her stud-worthy beast.

"I will relieve your stress," I told Spelon, then realized the sexual connotations of what I'd just said. "I mean, I have news to impart."

"Divulge us, old woman," Tenor said, somehow giving me the impression that he could see into my thoughts of a moment before.

I might have blushed. My face heated. I looked away, avoiding his gaze. Too much testosterone in this residence, I told myself. I needed to visit Tem and get a quick realignment.

"I doubt you have heard that Tem had a big meeting in the Great Hall, inviting all the Priestesses, I began . . ."

Her hunky guy looked quite relieved to hear the outcome. The other two looked thoughtful, but Shaara was horrified.

"The Saberey won't eat her, will they?" the girl asked, looking worried.

"Who knows," I said. "They do as they wish. You know that. But the significant part is that it will be hands-off you, Shaara. No one will ever dare harass you again."

"They better not," Spelon said, "Or this time, I will . . ."

"No, you won't," Shaara said, clasping his hand and squeezing until he met her gaze. "Ouch?" he said when we all knew that her grip hadn't the least impact on his mighty hand.

She laughed, which is exactly what he wanted.

I remembered vividly how gruff he used to be. She'd complained about him constantly, irritated by his overly domineering manner. None of that here. She had completely tamed the maddening beast.

It was an interesting morning. As I rose up, ready to journey with them to the Institute, I thought about transitions, changes, and how maybe there was hope for the Shapechanger.

# Tenor

I found out how to make an appointment with Tem. Once contacted I was told I did not need one, just to come in. Apparently, that was one of perks of being family. Sitting in a chair, sipping that horrible hot cider-caff substance, we chatted for a moment of inconsequentials. I had brought little Shaarac with me this time. With ample guards, thanks to Tem, the others had not objected.

The child sat at the table with us, sipping something that looked much more inviting than what I'd gotten. He was given cookies, too, a fact of which he seemed very taken with. They had colorful speckles on them, which he was tonguing off. I wondered if he would end with a rainbow-speckled tongue, but no matter.

I asked about news of Altar. Shaarac lifted his head, set down the cookie, and waited, like me, hoping to hear something good we could take back to Shaara. Or, in his case, perhaps, information about his father. There had been no contact even though a tenTide had passed since we had last spoken. There was no news.

The next item was about Shaara and the Institute. She was doing well or said she was. There had, to our knowledge, been no more disagreeable incidents. Shaara seemed content, even cheerful, most of the time.

Then, I came to the subject I had intended to address all along. I told Tem about the landoor ranch.

"Landoor?" he said, stroking his jaw. "I remember something Shaarvan said once."

Shaarac was back to tongue-swabbing his cookie. He looked up and said, "Shaarvan is my daddy, my real daddy."

"Yes," Tem said. "I know. He is my nephew. His daddy is my brother."

"Oh," Shaarac said. He put his cookie back on the plate and set his elbows on the table, leaning in to ponder that. "Everyone has a mommy and daddy. I have one mommy and four or five daddies. Is Tren a daddy?" he asked me.

I was not sure how to answer that. I nodded. "He wants to be a daddy like Spelon, Tenor, and me, I said. "Is that okay?"

Shaarac nodded. He seemed to like that idea.

"I used to have another daddy, but he went into space in a capsule. He wanted to see a star."

Tem smiled at the boy fondly. "Yes. Stegthal went to rest on a star. That was his wish, your mommy said."

"I wish he had stayed with us, but he got mean. I wish my other daddies on Altar would come see us. They played with me. We played ball. Thaandar could not. He drops the ball. Do you know how to play ball?"

I wanted to discuss the landoors, but Shaarac trumped that conversation. Our ball toss turned into a three-way.

After a while, Tem sat down, saying he was tired. Shaarac went back to his cookie, and I revived the conversation about the landoors. "If I wanted to buy a landoor, how would I go about doing so? You said we had unlimited funds, but does that include the price of an expensive landoor? If the owner is willing to sell him, of course."

"Ah," Tem said. "The reason for this delightful visit."

Tem ordered more of the tongue-lashing beverage, then sat a moment in thought. When our fresh orders came, along with a new cookie for Shaarac, one with even more of the colored sprinkles, Tem said, "The funds, as I said before, are unlimited. However, what will happen when your departure to Altar arrives? That could be any minute — or a Pass away. What would happen to the landoor then? Would it not be better if the animal were simply leased or rented?"

Shaarac brought me a licked cookie to sample. I took a bite. He returned to his chair with the rest of it.

"I want to go to Altar," Shaarac said. "Daddy Shaarvan lives there. Daddy Tren, too. Mommy wants to go to Altar, too. Thaandar does not. He is too little. He can come, though. But he does not get a choice. He is a baby. He does not talk except to say things like mmm which means milk or Mom. I cannot tell, but Mommy knows."

"Yes," I agreed with Shaarac. That is all true. One day, we will go to Altar, and we'll see your daddies."

Shaarac wiggled off his chair and went to sit with Tem. I am not sure the Shapechanger had ever had a child sitting in his lap, but he did it well. No fuss.

"The landoor would be a gift from us," I continued. "We want to give Shaara a present."

"Then, do so. I have no objections, but she will cry when she must leave him."

"Mommy cries lots. Spelon says all mommies cry."

"I suppose," Tem said. "Maybe they cry because they are happy to have such a fine son, two fine sons."

"Yes," Shaarac said, but he wiggled off Tem's lap and went back to his cookie-licking. His interest in the conversation had ended.

I stood and prepared to depart, but the walls started shadowing me. Having heard the details of the meeting with the Priestesses, I watched in fascination as the shadows turned into the images of four Saberey staring down at us.

"This is Shaarac, son of Shaarvan?" one asked.

I was busy bowing to the Saberey, but Shaarac let go of my hand and walked closer. "I am Shaarac. Do you know my daddy?"

The great She-cat smiled down at him. "You are a fine little fellow. You will prowl the forest with us soon, will you not?"

He laughed. "In Altar? With Daddy. Mommy can come, too, right?"

"Yes. Your mommy must come. She is a Trendacons like you."

"Spelon, Thedar, and Tenor are Trendacons, too, now. But Tessa is not. I do not know if Tren is a Trendacons, but he is a daddy. Can *all* my daddies come?"

The She-cat seemed enchanted with Shaarac. She left the wall and came down to sit beside him.

"Can I pet you?" Shaarac asked, forgetting his question in his delight at the nearness of the big cat.

"You may do so. Is this one of your other daddies?" she asked, looking at me.

I gulped, then stepped forward. "I am Tenor," I said, "Bondmate and guardian to Shaara."

"You may touch me," she said.

To touch a Saberey. I could die in contentment. Thedar will be jealous. Three steps forward, and I, too, petted the huge cat. Her fur was like velvet, like the inner thigh of a woman.

Tem, not forgotten in all this, came closer. "What is the news from Altar?" he asked.

"Shaarvan has not yet relented. He is not cold to her. He thinks to sacrifice himself for her happiness. He deceives himself."

Tem nodded, but he was smiling. "We Shapechanger are all fools when our mates are involved."

The She-cat yawned, her teeth sharp and long, but she was careful not to endanger Shaarac. She began to purr.

"Shaarvan must rebuild his house. He must prepare for the return of Shaara of Shaarvan. We do not like this separation. It has been too long."

"He has not contacted us of late. Perhaps you can urge him to . . ."

"This is taxing. I must leave now. We have not been talking to the heir, but we will do so. Goodbye, little Shaarac, Tenor."

I bowed to her and to the others, and they were all suddenly gone. The walls were again only a white surface as if the cats had been nothing but a mirage. I blinked, wondering if I'd imagined it. But Tem and Shaarac had seen the Saberey. They were still staring at the wall.

"Will the cats come back?" Shaarac asked.

Tem nodded. "Perhaps you will walk the forest with them soon. You are a very fortunate young Shapechanger."

"But not Thaandar? Will he get to come with us? Can he see the cats, too?"

"One Tide," Tem said as he kissed Shaarac goodbye.

# Shaara

My bondmates have gifted me with Mandar. They said it was for my birthPass, but I'd long ago lost track of that. I think I am twenty-three... The years were different on Earth. Here, they flow, in a crazy system I've never learned. I can't reckon it by my sons' ages because Shaarac had been put into deep sleep for the entire time I was in Freinana. But whether it was or wasn't my birthTide, I pretended it was.

Besides, the Shapechanger never counted birthTides. Their longer lives meant that they stayed for an indeterminate time in good health, physically at their peak. The age of my bondmates was actually as much a mystery as their early histories. The only tell came with Tenor, whose hair had spots of white, yet I don't believe the white hairs had increased since I'd known him.

But they'd given me Mandar, bought from his owner, and now the landoor was mine. Happiness filled my heart to overflowing. I kissed every one of my bondmates and hugged them, too. Plus, Shaarac and

Thaandar for good measure. My joy had no bounds except for the eternal ache, the one always with me, because my soul missed Shaarvan. But on such a wondrous Tide, even his lack couldn't spoil my fun.

The owner had agreed to continue his care of Mandar, feeding him and making sure he had the freedom of the pen during the fiveTide when I was busy at the Institute. It was all too perfect. I felt like dancing and did, much to the delight of my sons, who joined in, as did my formerly stern and slightly stiff bondmates.

Then, we started off on our long walk to the ranch, or at least we would have if Spelon hadn't stopped me to hand me another present. He'd given me a pair of pants, long pants, the kind just right for riding. He got a deeper kiss than the others for that. My inner thighs had chapped before, something he'd been very miffed about. Riding without a proper buffer between saddle and rider was not a comfortable experience.

Spelon told me I'd have to wait until we reached the ranch to wear them, a sensible precaution since we still got numerous looks from young Shapechanger. But although we hadn't been bothered since Tem's additional guards, pants on a female might be the flame to a fire.

I still had not gotten the males to try out riding, but Shaarac enjoyed the *old chair* Toron called Stuba. Shaarac liked the name of the landoor since he still remembered the donkey-goat stubras we'd adopted on Deathstar.

Spelon had discovered on an earlier excursion that Toron kept weights and an exercise mat, as well as various other mechanisms for muscle torture. Both Tenor and Thedar had bought books. Toron supplied us with an old cabinet drawer that substituted perfectly for a crib when Thaandar was ready to nod off. It was everything we needed, and I had Mandar all to myself. I quickly changed, finding the pants a perfect fit. Spelon knew me well, obviously.

I worked out the landoor's energy, always first on the agenda, so he'd listen, then I set to work, determined to teach him the basics of dressage. He and I worked on simple circles and a bit on leg yield. He was an apt learner. He wanted to please me.

At various times, I felt the presence of Tem's guards. They never stayed in one place long. They were hard to spot, too. My bondmates rotated in their supervisory position. I could always feel one of them checking on me. But no one bothered me except Shaarac, who constantly wanted up on Stuba and back down again. Usually, Thedar or Tenor would handle that. The podo creature was a draw at any time. Stick throwing and retrieval had joined ball throwing and catching as a favorite activity. If only Shaarac's attention span wasn't so short.

It was after I'd finished most of my lessons with Mandar that Tem showed up. He wasn't one to leave his Great Hall often. He had done so more often since we'd arrived on Westla than ever before, according to Tessa. But the sight of him outside the arena was a big surprise.

I was only walking Mandar by then, having finished most of the exercise work, so Tem didn't get to see how wonderful my landoor was, but I suppose to one who'd never seen a landoor before, fancy equitation probably meant little.

As if trumpets were playing to announce Tem's sudden presence at the ranch, the males almost instantly appeared, Tenor with the baby and Thedar holding the lead rope of Stuba with Shaarac back in the saddle. Tem's eyes moved from me to my son.

"Where are your landoors?" he asked my bondmates.

"We'll ride if you will," Tenor said, laughing.

Toron, slower than my guys to feel the potent Power of the Head of Westla setting foot on his property, made his way rather slowly toward us. "Great one," Toron said when he reached Tem. "Welcome to my ranch. I am honored."

"Toron, first greetings," Tem said politely. "I think it is time for the riders to take a break. Would you kindly escort the landoors away?"

My son didn't like that, but he didn't argue. Perhaps he felt the tendrils of magic emitting from Tem as most Shapechanger did. But more likely, he remembered Tem from his last visit with Tenor. When my son was lifted down from Stuba, he turned to look up at Tem and said, "Toron has a podo. He gets sticks when you throw them."

"Delightful," Tem said, giving him a smile that showed little impatience for the delay in spending a moment with his grandnephew, although the others and I could feel something brewing inside him. Was there news from Altar? Had Tessa foreseen something?

I itched to demand he tell us, but I kept still, only joining my hand to Spelon's, I think because I was too cowardly to hear what Tem had to say without support.

"Is there a place to sit down?" Tem asked, his eyes noting my movement, surveying the others while still appearing to give Shaarac the attention he was demanding. No wonder Tem was the head of Westla.

Tenor and Thedar led us toward the rest area. There was none of the *Cha* that Tem liked, but he accepted a cold fruit drink and managed to say hello, at Shaarac's request, to the podo at the same time. Tem even tossed a stick for the podo, much to the child's great delight.

"Can we play ball?" Shaarac wanted to know, tugging on Tem's fancy and previously immaculate dress shirt.

I would have chided my son, but Thedar stepped in first, telling Shaarac how Shapechanger waited quietly until the time was right for interaction. "They never touch another without permission."

I could have said something snippy about how that didn't apply to their treatment for girls, but I astutely followed Thedar's gesture of admonition when he caught my thought. I was supposed to be better at not projecting. I was better with it at the Institute, but with my bondmates, it was more difficult. Either I let down my defenses, or they just knew me too well.

Maybe such treatment of girls no longer applied to me since I'd proven my ability to kill a Shapechanger, but there were hundreds of thousands of girls who . . .

"Shaara, you are projecting," Tenor said.

Whoops. I built up the interior wall I was learning to create and shot a glance at the males. They were all regarding me with various expressions. Spelon looked almost humbled. Thedar sighed and shook his head, as usual, viewing me like the father of a mischievous child. Tenor. Okay, he was poker-faced.

Not so Tem, who was staring at me like some great work of art, admiration in his eyes. I glanced over at Shaarac. Thankfully, he hadn't ridden the currents of my rebellious thought. He was busy playing with the podo.

I dropped my eyes and eyed my hand, enveloped in Spelon's huge mitt. He squeezed, then dabbed a kiss on my cheek. His eyes had reverted to his normal, slightly mocking aspect. I knew that was the view he projected from habit.

It was his default face, half for show, half because the reality was that he was physically stronger than anyone else and used to being the eye candy for any female that came into his orb. I guess cocky suited him.

He laughed, picking up some of what I was thinking even with my wall at its staunchest. But then, we were touching, which made it harder to keep my thoughts from leaking outward.

I pushed at his arm. "You didn't need to read me, you big bully," I said, only partially in jest.

"I have heard from Altar," Tem said, breaking through everything, streamlining to the essence of the meeting. He took out a piece of paper, something rarely used in Westla. He unfolded it and read:

"Tevor is still in a coma. Teea is deep in grief. Send Shaara with the boys. She can soothe Teea. I assume Thal will be willing to fly you here. A battalion will meet your ship for safety. *Shaarvan.*"

"He doesn't know about Thal," I said, devastated because I realized that someone would have to tell him. Shaarvan might be disappointed, even angry with the guy, but they'd once been good friends.

"Thal's ship is yours now, Shaara," Tem said. "You were legally his wife. In fact, I should have told you before. All of his possessions and funds, which are substantial, now belong to you."

As if I wanted his pile of books and telescopes. But then what Tem said finally sank in. "Wait, I thought a woman couldn't own anything — like all that money I earned in a card game with my bondmates."

The males laughed. "Too late to claim it now," Tenor said, looking smug.

Tem snorted, probably having heard the story about me being involved in a card game. Thal hadn't been happy about it. He'd told me that it was inappropriate behavior for a woman.

"It is different now," Tem told me. "You are a Priestess. Your rights are almost equivalent to a Shapechanger's."

That was enlightening. The males hadn't bothered to inform me about that before.

"Isn't she also the Queen of Altar?" Thedar asked. "If so, does she own any property on that planet? Are we tied to a very, very wealthy woman — a rich Priestess, I mean."

They were all smiling broadly, teasing me, I think, but maybe not. They were each displaying the typically unemotional and inscrutable Shapechanger face of a male who didn't want you to read him.

"But does she not belong to Shaarvan officially, so everything actually belongs to him?" Spelon asked.

As if someone had tossed a stun net over us, silence descended. I'd thought my guardians' expressions were unreadable before, but someone had just erased even the hint of humor in their eyes. Talk about a blank slate.

I heaved a giant breath and watched Shaarac toss the stick again, his rather longish hair creeping down into his eyes. I needed to ask Tenor to trim it. I'd volunteer, but I knew they wouldn't allow me to cut it. I sometimes thought they believed Shaarac was more theirs than mine.

Blocking out Spelon's question since it was entirely unimportant, I closed my eyes and reviewed Shaarvan's letter. Something about it bothered me. No. Everything bothered me about it. It seemed wrong. Its shortness. Its coldness.

Of course, Shaarvan hadn't said he missed me. I was persona non grata. But he hadn't said he missed the boys either. No greeting to his Shapechanger friends, my guardians. He hadn't even said anything to his uncle. Had he become aloof with even them?

"Could you read the letter again, Tem. Please?" I said.

The second time, my alarm was even worse. What Shaarvan had written was about as welcome as giving someone a prickly cactus when you knew they wanted a fragrant flower. Nothing forthcoming. Nothing personal. What did it mean? Had the war turned Shaarvan into a robot male?

I questioned the others. It didn't seem as obvious to them. "Perhaps he was in a hurry," Tenor said.

I nodded. I had no concept of what war was like. Perhaps Shaarvan was dodging bullets, although Thal had told me the war on Altar was not like that. More like a concentrated mental activity, pressing against the desire of the Commoners, making them want to turn around and head home.

But if that were so, why had Shaarvan said there'd be a platoon when our ship landed? Didn't that imply that warlike maneuvers were still occurring?

And even if the letter wasn't strange, what did I do about the Institute? I hadn't attended long enough to control my Power. I was still leaking emotions, as the males had indicated a moment ago. I wasn't ready.

But it didn't matter. There was no question I'd be going. Even if Shaarvan didn't want me around, I'd be close to him. I'd see him, and maybe . . .

I couldn't think of that now.

"When do we leave?" I asked. Is the ship ready for departure? Do we need to get supplies or load it with fuel, or . . ."

"We will handle that, Shaara," Thedar said. "But are you sure you want to go? Just because Teea needs you, is that enough reason to put yourself into a situation where your heart will be broken again?"

The stern, impassive faces that had been neutralized to prevent my reading them were now open. They were concerned and caring.

"Mommy, I'm hungry. Can we go home now?" Shaarac said. As if that had produced some magical synchrony between the brothers, Thaandar opened his mouth and let out an angry wail.

Thedar lifted Thaandar out of the crib drawer we used at the ranch and patted his bottom. I could tell by the sag that it was time for a change, but Thedar hadn't looked before he touched. His face twisted with a combination of dismay and disgust. Then, without a word, he carted Thaandar off to the necessary room. Of course, Thedar had spare potty pants. He always did. Tenor usually had some, too.

Spelon in the childcare department was lacking... He worried more about weapons and guarding me than changing diapers or offering bottles.

We stood up. Tem gave me a final nod. "So you will be going?" he asked me. "I would appreciate it if you would hold off a fiveTide. I want to send a medic with you for Tevor."

"From the Institute?"

"No. Altar is not very receptive to the Priestesses. You need to know that, Shaara. They grant no freedoms to Priestesses in Altar."

"Even for their Queen?" Spelon asked, shaking his head in disbelief.

Tem sighed. "I have absolutely no idea what is going on there. But if you get into any trouble that Shaarvan cannot get you out of, I, personally, will come get you with a whole fleet of ships that they will not be able to say no to. You are family now, my favorite niece. These boys, Tenor, Thedar, you, Spelon, and you, Shaara. You are all Trendacons. My family. Never forget that."

"Also, Shaara, remember the Saberey. They will defend you from danger. Call on them in your mind. They will always show up for you. They told me so."

Tem left then. Tenor returned with Thaandar. I wanted to dart into the stable to say good-bye to Mandar, but Tem probably had a good reason for asking us to wait a fiveTide. I'd probably get to return to the ranch before we left.

I wished I had said good-bye to my landoor and to Toron. A fiveTide goes by too rapidly. I didn't make it back to see Mandar before we were heading to the ship, Tessa and Tem accompanying us as far as the Space Port gate.

Good-byes are difficult. I hugged them, even grouchy Tessa, who had still not been able to foresee our future.

My sobs started, and Spelon helped me to continue walking despite my tear-blurry eyes. My resolution not to cry anymore was an impossible one to keep.

When we reached the ship, a strange woman, a Priestess from the feel of her, stood next to Thal's ship. Tenor greeted her and asked about her business there. We'd all forgotten Tem's request to take a medic to Tevor.

Why hadn't Tem mentioned the Priestess? Why had she met us at the ship and not at the gate where Tem could more properly introduce her? And hadn't he said that he wouldn't send a Priestess?

I had a pile of questions to ask, but I swallowed them. We were heading for Altar. That was the most important thing. Soon, I would see Shaarvan. No matter what happened, currents of anticipation were running up and down my spine. I leaned into Spelon, hoping he wasn't picking up my thoughts, but of course, he was.

"I understand my darling one. You are bonded. I know you are his forever. But you can still love me, too, right? A little?"

He got a kiss for that, a really good one, so good in fact, Tenor and Thedar had to yell at us to break it up and get into the ship so we could blast off. Shaarac, Thaandar, and Tem's medic friend had already boarded. We were the last to walk up the ramp.

The Great Eye of the Saberey opened to allow our passage. That was my favorite part. After that, I figured the flight would be as dull as porridge. I was wrong. Tura changed everything.

# *Chapter Eleven*

## Shaara

The moment Spelon and I walked up the ramp and shut the doors, the ship blasted off into and through the Great Saberey Eye. Moments later, everyone was heading for their quarters and for bed. I didn't really get to meet Tura until that next morning.

I had planned to do some studying once on shipboard, but Spelon had other plans. His plans were enjoyable. No complaints. And again in the morning, he made us late. We were the last to join the others for our first meal together.

Thedar and Tenor teased me about our tardiness, then complained about the smell they said still lingered about us, but Spelon and I had showered. Twice. It was Spelon's fault. He had a way of looking at me, a certain look in his eyes, that set my body to thinking thoughts unacceptable around the others, especially with my sons present. And the Priestess Tula.

But in spite of that complication, I grabbed a look at her, a good look. I thought she appeared younger than she had the evening before. She was no crone but a middle-aged woman with a fine figure and mid-length blond-brown hair, which on Earth was called dirty blonde. It looked good on her.

Plus, she had the deep gray eyes of Power but accompanied by a rather sensual, come-hither look, which, from observing Thedar, was actively working. Definite vibes there. I hoped their potential pairing didn't upset Tenor. If he was the only one left out of night fun, it might get awkward.

Tura seemed open and friendly with me. There was no snobbish attitude or frown because I was young. I supposed in picking her, Tem and Tessa had made sure of her receptivity for who and what I was prior to inviting her to share a ship with us.

She seemed to be a child person, too. I'd noticed that not all Priestesses were. Some of them had put maternal instincts into their past history and no longer wanted to be reminded of such things. Interaction with a small child offering a possibly grimy hand to hold or listening to a story where you had to interpret the meanings between the lines wasn't everyone's cup of *Cha*, understandably.

But Tura took to Shaarac right away, telling him she would love to play toss with him later. She even offered to teach him a couple of variations. He wasn't sure what variations meant, but he seemed open to it. He started in telling her all about the podo who retrieved sticks and Stuba, who was just like the small animals on Deathstar that used to give him rides.

"Tenor and Thedar give me rides, too," Shaarac said, and there was that look on the Priestess' face again as she made goo-goo eyes, first at Thedar and then at Tenor.

"I should like to get some rides, too," Tura said.

Beside me, Spelon almost dropped his cup of *Kla*, the drink all of us preferred to *Cha*. Spelon's eyes flashed to me, and he raised one eyebrow most expressively.

Meanwhile, I was giving baby Thaandar his bottle and admiring his adorable fat cheeks, so it was hard for me to watch the expressions of the males. But the currents buzzing about the room were heated. The air took on a sweet scent. Sugar actually had no odor, but it was as if a taste of its sweetness lingered on the back of my tongue. I guess that described an aroma as much as a taste. But, it was permeating the room. It was going to be a very, very odd flight to Altar.

"Could I hold the baby?" Tura asked.

I glanced at the others but saw no negation. They seemed willing to trust Thaandar to the unknown woman. I smiled at her and handed him over.

Thaandar looked back at me, probably puzzled by the movement in the middle of his breakfast, but then he calmly fastened his attention to the new face. For a moment, the milk bubbled about his lips, dripping down on Tura's dress. She took it with composure, not gasping or otherwise indicating that a baby's overflow onto her gown was disturbing. In fact, she laughed.

"He is a fine little Shapechanger, is he not?"

Okay, she'd just won my support. I agreed with her, picked up a piece of compressed bread, and bit into it.

"Tell me about your instructional needs, Shaara. Tem said that I should work with you on the way to Altar."

My sip of *Kla* slipped sideways, going down. I coughed. Spelon tried to pat my back. Only his back slaps were fierce enough to send me half out of my chair. I halted that action, pulled in air, and got my thoughts back into gear.

"I would love to work with you," I told Tura, but I'm sure you'll agree that a discussion of my Priestess business must remain . . ."

"Of course," she said, laughing softly. "But I figured that as incapable of curbing your projection as you are, your guardians would already know many of our deepest secrets."

Seeing my reaction to what I saw as an insult, Tura raised her hand. "No, do not misinterpret. No offense was meant. It is what it is, Shaara. You do the best you can, but you are young. It is a failing of youth, not of you personally."

She laughed, then lifted Thaandar up and placed him over her shoulder for a proper burping.

"I miss having a baby. My only son and my husband were both killed by Gregar pirates. I was rescued after considerable time being the captain's favorite . . ." She glanced over at Shaarac, but his interest was on assembling his *uvine* fruits into a military line. But ears often picked up things they were not obviously listening to. I appreciated Tura's skill at screening the details of her capture.

I nodded. "I spent time on Freinana in the same way,"

"Yes, we share that," she said, then smiled again, showing all the gestures of friendship.

I wanted to reach out, to accept her completely, but the Institute had taught me lessons of wisdom that made me cautious.

Tenor flashed a sign. Too quick for me to interpret if I even knew that particular Shapechanger gesture. But I assumed it meant to be cautious. I nodded infinitesimally.

Thedar reached out for the baby. "Thaandar will be exploding out the other end momentarily. It is best you hand him to me."

"I am not afraid of such things, my gallant one, but I suppose my moments of blissfully holding such sweetness must be shared."

Double meanings? I glanced at Tenor, but he avoided my glance. His face was in impassive mode, the default of Shapechanger males.

# Spelon

We had run into Tula's kind before. Many Priestesses were sex-starved players. Nothing wrong with that since Shapechanger were immune to the sexually transmitted diseases that Commoners were prone to. But it might be slightly awkward to engage in her proclivities on an enclosed ship with children and a Shapechanger wife, who by custom were always kept untainted by such carnal interests.

Of course, I was not one for overly sheltering Shaara. Our romps were full of excitement and hearty frolics, but I did not own Shaara. I must always be aware of that. So, our minglings were probably tame compared to what an experienced hedonistic explorer like Tura might bring to the bedroom.

Although I would not trade one second with Tura for what I shared with Shaara, I appreciated the fun that Thedar and Tenor might soon be having. They deserved it, too. Their drought these Passes had been long.

As to Shaara working with Tura, I had severe reservations. I would need to discuss that with the others. We usually did not feel the need to walk about inside the mind of a Priestess, something which was not entirely safe for males, but I wondered if, in this case, we should do so or at least observe Tura's training covertly. None of us could sense any lies within Tura, but she was still suspect. We had been tricked by Priestesses before, and Shaara was too precious to risk.

I would make sure I had the opportunity to separate myself from either Thedar or Tenor and discuss such things. I also thought it wise to require a watch on Tura's engagements with the children.

Supervised play would be fine, but alone time with them was something I distrusted.

# Tenor

Thedar was on me the moment I moved onto the ship's exercise mat. He stopped my pushups to let me know about his interaction with Tura. He gave it to me freely, no guilt about enjoying himself or holding back in case my feelings might be hurt because she had chosen him. As if. He also warned me that Tura would be slipping into *my* quarters for the same.

He looked thoughtful about that as if he hadn't made up his mind yet how he felt about such a rotation, but such things were not unknown with Priestesses. Those females could be very prolific in their needs. Besides, I joked that it would make our flight to Altar an interesting, fun fest.

Thedar was on watch with the two boys after Shaara finished her playtime with them. Although there was no firm scheduling yet, it would fall into place naturally soon enough. None of us resented spending time with our littles. Attending them was a delight.

Spelon was the next one to confront me. He seemed concerned about Thedar's willingness to dally with a stranger while onboard the ship. I assured him that I had already discussed the situation with Thedar and that he was aware that dalliance did not preclude vigilance.

I agreed with Spelon's concern for the children's safety, but I had qualms about observing Priestess lessons.

"What would Tessa say?" I asked him.

Both of us shivered instinctively. We had been aware of her wondering thoughts that Tide over breakfast. Such pseudo-suggestions were the equivalent of an offer to bed that small cat of hers. Claws and fangs with Power dribbling out her pores. No takers.

The possibility remained that Tura might be similar, but our trip was not a long one. Surveillance and caution would serve us well.

"And about the supervision of Shaara's instruction?" Spelon asked, still worrying over that aspect.

"Yes, I agree on its necessity. Even if we later have to deal with Tessa," I said. "We need to oversee all Tura's private moments with Shaara. Tura will know, of course. Hopefully, the deepest secrets will be kept inviolate."

Spelon left then, giving me time to think. Musings over the situation were obviously not to be. My pushups were once more put on hold because the object of the recent discussion dropped in.

"Ah, an exercise room. How quaint," Tura purred.

I sat up, grabbed two of the heavier weights, and started on my arm muscles, ignoring Tura as much as possible. I hoped she'd use the lesser weights and allow me some peace, but that wasn't her intention.

She strode over to me in a rather catlike manner, her hips swaying in the way females adopt for hunter mode. I was prepared for her approach but not for the touch of her hand on the muscles of my arm. Her grasp was not tight nor adversarially predatory, but it was intentionally erotic. All qualms about her good will temporarily slurred into background noise as my testes firmed and heated, and my rod grew its bone.

The Priestess, with a mere look at the door, bolted it shut. She stripped off her skin-tight red dress and waved it like a flag for a moment before tossing it aside. Her skin turned young, her breasts lifted, and her face shed lines and shadows. She was glorious, a full flower of femininity. I set down the weights and took full advantage of Tura's offering.

# Shaara

I wandered about the ship driftingly. Thaandar had gone to sleep. Thedar was now with Shaarac, giving him instructions on being a male Shapechanger. My presence hadn't been welcome for that. Apparently, there were still secrets I was not allowed to know.

Spelon was off in Thal's former study, working on something. Spelon had never been much of a book reader, but since we returned to Westla, his head was often bent over one. Thedar had told me Spelon was taking classes. It worried me that our trip to Altar would disturb that. I wondered if Spelon had considered staying on Westla, but he'd made no mention of it.

Was I selfish, forcing my guardians to make their lives always about me? Yet, wasn't their pledge originally to Shaarvan? Maybe it was Shaarvan's letter that had sent them zooming off to Altar and not me at all. When he received the boys, would Shaarvan release my guardians from their bond, leaving me alone? Another worry to add to my list. I seemed to collect worries like seashells. Although I'd love to empty my pockets of them and toss them back on the beach, they lingered, attached to me, obviously.

Once upon a time, when I was a new wife, Shaarvan had repeatedly told me that I must only and always obey the Primary: *Please your husband.*

Had life been simpler then with only that one worry? I was never good at following the Primary, and I had chosen to discard it completely when I became a Priestess. As much as I wanted Shaarvan, I knew I could not go back to that earlier time. I shrugged, took in several deep breaths, then shook my head at my thoughts. As Tessa always said, "Looking backwards for a brief time was okay, but walking backwards was rarely beneficial for good balance."

I decided to take some exercise mat time. That would make Spelon happy. He was always telling me I didn't get adequate workouts. But when I went to the ship's gym, the door was locked. Priestess locked.

So Tura was working out. But why had she barred the rest of us from entry? She hadn't acted shy earlier.

I mentally shrugged, then made my way back to the room I shared with Spelon. A book from the Institute was open to the page I'd been working on. Another spell to learn and a lecture on the mechanics of Power to read. I studied the syllabus sent with me. Tessa had not given me any Tides off. I set to work. Feeling sorry for myself, since I'd been deserted by everyone, I had trouble concentrating. What would Tessa say?

# Spelon

I was alone in the study, trying to read a book. The Priestess Tura entered and invaded my space. She wore the smell of Tenor and reeked of sex hormones — not exactly a repulsive odor to a Shapechanger, but not a welcome one in this situation.

I turned from my book to look at her.

"Tired of Thedar and Tenor already?" I said contemptuously.

"When mouth-watering desserts fill the display case of a restaurant, does one bother with vegetables?" she asked in a cheeky manner.

I closed my book and gave up on studying. I decided to put this unasked-for visit to good use. I had questions to ask, and she seemed to be in a mood to give me anything I wanted. But just to make sure she didn't confuse talking with foreplay, I thought I'd straighten her out on my intentions.

"I belong to Shaara."

Tura took another step toward me. I stopped her with a Shapechanger gesture. It was obvious that she had once been properly trained. She halted, then considered me, probably ascertaining whether I might be more than she could handle.

"Do you truly belong to her?" Tura questioned but did not come closer. "Possibly, at least for the moment, but she belongs to Shaarvan. Sounds rather like a triangular situation, does it not?"

The Priestess' eyes were shading to green. I partially changed. When a Shapechanger did that, nothing a Priestess attempted could ever touch us.

"What are your intentions with Shaara? Are you a friend or a foe?" I demanded, trusting the female even less than when she had first boarded the ship.

"I will not harm any of you. Tessa asked me to go to Altar. I will see if I can improve the health of Tem's brother."

I waited, watching her face for signs that she had lied. She had no reaction, so she was being truthful.

"Yet, there is more to you than you admit," I said. "You have entered this room to attempt seduction, yet you claim to want to assist Shaara, to be her friend even."

"I will be. She needs one, but I do not see why I shouldn't enjoy the trip to Altar. You are a prize worth a bit of risk."

"No."

"Oh, surely there is no harm in sampling desserts. Who would lose out? Not Shaara. She doesn't need to know."

Strange that Tura's husband had been Shapechanger. She seemed completely unaware of the Shapechanger protocol.

Tura laughed. "My husband was a long time ago. I have forgotten those days. No need to remember.

"I used to be Tem's lover, but he didn't share well. I don't know if that counts as being his friend. Tessa has been my friend even longer. She'd like me to join her Institute, but it's filled with rigid old gossips. I have refused her many times and will continue to do so. I prefer living in Zandors, a *spotcar* away from West. There, I can rule the town as I like with my many playmates."

She rattled on like a Commoner female. Interesting. I couldn't quite figure her out. She confused me, but not in a way that would ever injure Shaara. I would never do anything to hurt my little warrior.

"But you wanted to travel to Altar?" I said. "A war zone now and a place where Priestesses receive little respect. Why?"

"I get bored easily. Altar is different. Since my husband and son died, I've been adrift. But I like muscles a lot. I especially like what I see among you three. After Altar has lost its sparkle, perhaps you'd like to visit me in Zandors."

"I see," I said, although I did not. "I expect it is time for your instruction with Shaara. Perhaps you would prefer a shower first. She is very intuitive with scents. She might find it upsetting that you have decided to feast so liberally on her two older guardians."

"Indeed? So she lays claim to all three of you?"

"Yes."

"I cannot respect that, I'm afraid. I have needs."

"So I see, or rather smell."

"I could fit you in right now. It would be cozy among your books and telescopes."

"I have work to do. I presume we will share your company at the next meal."

I turned my attention from her and looked down at my book, hoping that would be enough to dissuade her. She sighed loudly, petulantly, but a moment later, the door opened and closed, and when I looked up, the room was empty again. It took much longer for her ugly stench to entirely dissipate.

# Tura

I did not appreciate Spelon's rejection. I had waited a long time to find a suitable Shapechanger to replace my Tyran. Spelon met all my requirements, other than he wasn't currently available . . . But he would be soon.

Priestesses did not usually take on permanent lovers, but I was rather the exception. I had a very pleasant group of them, among whom I rotated at whim. Most of them had been suitably trained. They no longer believed they could do their Shapechanger training on me. In fact, the moment they tried to domineer, I ousted them except in the bedroom. Male dominance could be fun in sex play.

I had just kicked out a feisty but extremely virile young Shapechanger who had not been able to play by my rules. Tyran had been a lovely piece of art, but his continual attempts of control were just not acceptable. He ordered me to obey him one time too many. I ordered him to leave.

My other males, all marble-chested sex gods with perfect shoulder, arm, and waist circumferences and not an ounce of fat on any of them, gave me something to look at, especially when I wandered into my weight room. Several would often be on the wrestling mat, writhing and stretching their lovely muscles, while others would be working weights, sweat dripping down their backs.

But Tyran had been special, and when I was forced to give him the boot, depression set in. I missed his powerful control in the bedroom and the way he and I were constantly verbally sparring. I missed the heft of his warm, powerful body. As everyone knows, life without challenge swiftly grows tedious.

When Tessa had first written about Spelon, I perked up. Her descriptions of him, the muscular curvature of arms that were solid with strength, and the lurid nature of Tessa's writing as she related such things intrigued me. Yes, I was sure that Spelon could be the one I hungered for, the one who could end my depression over the loss of Tyran.

But it was the last letter that Tessa sent that raved over the changes from Spelon's former gruffness to his present willingness to cater to his girl's desires that convinced me to make the trip to Altar with them. Affability in a Shapechanger Warrior Lord was absolutely unknown.

Yes, I would enjoy playing with Tenor and Thedar. Both were jewels that would spice up my collection if I could pry them away from their girl. Adding them to my harem would improve the academics of my group. A little philosophy and intellectual conversation would smooth over the current lack I was feeling in my sexual ensemble. But Spelon . . . I licked my lips and thought about the strength of his arms, the thickness of those thighs. Spelon was every woman's fantasy, and he would soon be mine if I had anything to say about it.

Not wishing to disappoint, I returned to my room, showered, and prepared to enchant their little princess.

I was aware that Shaara was supposedly the anointed one of the Trendacons. Even the Sabereys adored her. Hopefully, that meant that her Power was as deep as Tessa said. But the girl's youth was such a handicap. No one that age could attain control over the raging fires of Power.

The vast amounts of energy that soared through a Priestess' body necessitated a firm, mature hold, something that tiny speck of a girl couldn't possibly have. But I'd promised Tessa I would try, no matter how fruitless I believed it to be.

Besides, I couldn't be in bed with two potent Shapechanger males every moment of the Tide. Anticipation would roast the meat to a higher flame. Yum.

# Shaara

Two of my guardians entered my room. Thedar was looking sweaty. I presumed he'd been exercising. Spelon was rubbing his eyes, probably from studying too much.

I turned around to present a more receptive posture, wondering what this was about. Obviously, I was in trouble about something. What had I done this time?

But then it hit me. I was a Priestess. They wouldn't have come in to lecture me.

"Are the boys alright?" I asked.

Spelon walked over to massage my shoulders. "The boys are fine," he said. "But we need to talk with you about Tura."

"Okay." I glanced at Thedar. Was he going to admit that he and Tura were . . ."

"We do not trust her, Shaara. You are not to spend time alone with her."

He was reverting to Shapechanger command, but I wouldn't criticize, not before hearing him out, at least.

"Spelon, how will that work if she's going to help me with the Priestess stuff?"

Thedar sat down on my bed. The room only had one chair, and I was sitting in it. I giggled. "Thedar, if you don't trust her, why are you playing *toesies* with her in your bedroom?"

Of course, they didn't know what that meant since I'd said *toesies* in English. I added, "bedding, joining, copulation . . ."

"Shaara!" Spelon exclaimed, cupping my mouth with his bear claw of a hand.

Thedar was silent a moment, appraising me. "We understand the meaning. Does it bother you, little one? Do you want us to stop?" Thedar asked.

"Us?" I shot a glance at Spelon. "You?"

Spelon shook his head. "No, my *Second*. I would not do that. I am fully yours."

I turned back to Thedar. "You mean you and Tenor. *Both* of you?"

"We will stop if it displeases you, Shaara."

Wow. This was a new concept for me. I mean, I hadn't thought about them as sexual beings. Not for a long time. How selfish of me.

"Maybe you can find someone on Altar. I'm sorry. It's my fault you don't have anyone. I bet Altar has an abundance of widows since there will be some who lost their husbands in the war."

I guess I'd started hanging my head, feeling guilty about my total oblivion to their needs. Thedar stood, came over to me, and lifted up my chin. "Never be sorry about our staying with you. We love you, Shaara. We would give our lives for you. But a little fun . . .well, if it doesn't offend you . . ."

I don't know what I would have said then. A knock sounded. For some reason, I assumed it was Tenor, but he was watching the boys.

Spelon called out, "Enter," and in strolled Tura.

"Oh, having a *bishquo*?" she asked.

It was a word I didn't know. I looked at Spelon, but he was busy glaring at Tura. I didn't think I needed to worry about him joining Tenon and Thedar. Spelon seemed pretty negative about Tura.

"You will watch your language," Thedar said. "Shaara is . . ."

"Yes, I know. A member of the elite, so preserving her innocence is a prime directive. Yes, I will keep it short and sweet, but do remember that she is the mother of two boys and was a slave on Freinana. A little exposure to the realities of life couldn't hurt her greatly."

Glares were flying. I'd heard that expression used once or twice among the Priestesses. Now I understood it. But the males' glower ratio after her short speech was a hundred percent.

Tura nodded as if she'd just confirmed something to herself. "Did you forbid Thedar from engaging in a nightly session of . . . um cards?"

I had to smile at that. "No, He and Tenor are free to play all the cards they want."

"Good," Tura said, fully understanding that I'd been informed of the nature of their card playing.

"Shall we begin our practice, Shaara?"

"Okay."

The prickly feeling of charged particles in the air dispersed, but the males didn't seem to want to leave. I remembered that Spelon had said I shouldn't be alone with Tura. But then, how was I to train with the Priestess?

Perhaps Tura understood what was going on. "It's a bit crowded in here. Perhaps we should move to the bigger room where we ate."

Everyone nodded.

And that is the reason my bandmates became the first males ever to be exposed to Priestess secrets. They watched every lesson, not speaking or intruding. I often forgot they were even there. I don't know if Tura did. She was ever watchful of the males, her eyes full of secrets that had nothing to do with my learning to control my Power.

# *Chapter Twelve*

## Tenor

It is a very good thing that Thal showed us how to fly his ship. It sometimes needed Shaara's imprint since she was the legal owner, but it allowed us to program the details. As Thal had said, it was an easy ship to navigate. We did little after that.

But we were approaching Altar, and I was unsure of the landing protocol. How did we announce ourselves? Where exactly should we land? I wished I knew as much about the ship's communications system as I did about the other basics of navigation.

I asked Shaara if she could contact Shaarvan, but she said he'd shut her out and never opened communications again. She couldn't feel Teea either, and, of course, Tevor was still in a coma.

I broached these worries with Thedar and Spelon. I was so desperate for answers I even asked Tura, expecting that she wouldn't know such details, but hoping that she might. I feared we might be stranded in space, hanging above the planet of our destination, unable to progress or to land.

What would happen if we zoomed into Altarian space without clearance? Would we be shot at? And if we survived that, could we land on someone else's empty spot at Space Port? I had no answers for such questions, and it worried me.

Should we announce that we were Trendacons? (If I knew how to do so.) Or was that a dangerous thing to admit? Shaarvan's letter had spoken of a platoon of soldiers that would be meeting us, but would public notification of our arrival be a death warrant? Was our arrival supposed to be a secret?

Even if the Commoners were the ones who met our ship, they wouldn't kill us. They wanted Shaara and her baby. But how would they know who we were? They might think we were Westlan forces coming to give battle.

"Do not frown so much," Shaara said, laying her hand on my arm. "They will not shoot us. Someone will see us floating up here and tell us what to do."

I could have slayed her innocence with derision. Such simplistic viewpoints of planetary defenses. But I said nothing. I turned, gazed down at her, and gave her a big smile. Her face looked radiant then. Perhaps she'd been afraid of my scorn.

I suppose in the past, we had treated her vilely, berating her for giving her opinions, casting her words into bins of discard as if she were Shaarac's age. What fools we had been. Why had we not perceived the keen mind inside her appealing body?

# Shaara

"Perhaps . . ." We all turned to look at Tura. If she had an idea, we were ready to listen. "What if Shaara and I directed our Power into some kind of announcement. Could the force of our joined efforts flow through space?"

"Shaara did that before at further distances," Spelon said.

"But I had a focal point then. It was always Shaarvan," I reminded him.

Tura nodded her head. "Then we keep him as our focus. We'll pound Shaarvan on the head with the strength of our combined will. Priestess Power."

"But what if he shuts us out?" I asked, not wanting to appear overly eager but admittedly slightly hopeful.

Tura grabbed me by the shoulders. "What do we have to lose, Shaara? Treat it like an exercise in focusing. Concentrate on getting into your husband's head, then ram him with Power."

Ram my Power at Shaarvan? Did they know what they were asking me? He'd turned away because I used my Power. This would make him twice as angry.

Thedar touched my shoulder to get my attention. "Shaara, what if you simply announce that his sons have arrived? He would not resent that."

Thedar was right. I kissed his cheek, then glanced at Tura. "Okay, that's perfect. How about a message that says. *Your sons are here. Guide us down.*"

Tura laughed. "Short and sweet. I love it. Okay take my hand so we can link. Build your energy like you're going to light a candle. Do you feel it heating up? Are your toes and fingers tingling? Feel the Power rushing from your feet up through your body. Let it shimmer back and forth, filling you. Now, Shaara."

*Your sons are here. Guide us down. Your sons are here. Guide us down.*

We kept on saying it over and over. Then Shaarac started yelling the words, and my bondmates joined in until we were all shouting it repeatedly.

At last, our voices gave out. We plopped down in chairs, drank some *Kla,* and waited.

"It doesn't matter if it didn't work this time. He might be busy. He might have ignored it. But we'll keep on . . ." Tura said. She broke off because, at that moment, we all heard Shaarvan's voice coming through the speaker.

"You crazy fools," Shaarvan said. "Where is Stegthal? I mean, Thal? Why is he not using the communicator to alert us?"

"Daddy?" Shaarac asked.

"Sh!" Spelon ordered him, his finger over his lips.

*We don't know how.* I thought back at him. *Thal is dead.*

"Who is with you, Shaara?" Shaarvan asked through the speaker.

*Spelon, Thedar, Tenor, and . . ."*

"Me, too. I am here," Shaarac said, forgetting Spelon's order. But it didn't matter because Shaarvan couldn't hear our words, only mind-speak.

"Okay, raise up the cover on the panel by the door. Locate the red button. It will open up the communication system. Thal hid it when you went into hiding. But you will see it light up. Then we can talk."

Tenor handed me the baby and then did as Sharvan had told us. I sank into a chair, drained from Power usage and from talking with Shaarvan.

"It was your idea," I said to Tura as she handed me some fruit juice. I reached for the cup and saw that my hands were shaking. Spelon noticed and took charge of Thaandar.

Tura told me to eat one of Shaarac's cookies to regenerate my Power. As I nibbled on one, Tura handed another to Shaarac.

"There," she said. "It is hard to be quiet sometimes, isn't it?"

My son nodded vigorously and then eyed Spelon. "I forget to be Shapechanger," Shaarac said.

Spelon ruffled his hair, then gave him a nod and a smile.

Once two-way was established, Thenor and Thedar were able to get all the directions we needed. With half an ear, I heard the conversation going on between Shaarvan, Thedar, and Tenor, but I knew I wouldn't be able to repeat a single bit of it. I was truthfully just listening to Shaarvan's voice, allowing it to flow through my body, absorbing the feelings it engendered.

Tura had told me about how the current should run up and down from my feet to my head, how it would fill every pore. I think that's exactly what I was feeling as the sound of Shaarvan's voice ricocheted throughout my body.

"Is she going to be okay?" Tura asked.

I heard her question. I heard Spelon say something back to her, but my brain had lifted up into the great gap between us, and I was zooming down to Shaarvan. At least, that's what it felt like. I'm glad I didn't actually do that. Shaarac would have gone hysterical, not to mention my bondmates and Tura, maybe.

But maybe Tura would have been glad to see me gone because she wanted Spelon, and the flow of scents emitting from her body was even stronger beside him than when she was near my other bondmates.

Should I protest? Did I have the right to, when all I wanted at that moment was to fly down to Altar, bow down to my husband, and beg him to take me back?

# Spelon

The moment I have been dreading was almost upon us. In minutes, we would land, and everything would be made known. Shaarvan would decide to take Shaara back, or he would reject her again. It was that simple. An on or off switch, with me in the middle.

If his response were yes, I would firm my backbone, smooth my face into impassivity, and pretend that his decision had no impact. I would watch Shaara walk away, leaving me in emptiness. And I would force myself to feel good about it because it was what would make her happiest.

Meanwhile, this hungry witch woman would think she had won. As if I were her prize, she was drooling over me. But the truth was that she disgusted me. I could never go from Shaara to a female like her. And I would never . . .

My thoughts were those of a story Shaara had once told us. A woman carrying eggs became so wrapped up in her ideas of what she would trade the eggs for that she forgot the eggs were in the basket on her head. She tilted her head, and the eggs all fell down.

I never understood why a female would be carrying eggs. Did she not have a male to carry them for her? And if she were a Commoner and had no husband, why would she put a basket of eggs on her head? Why and where could a female trade goods in public? So many concepts that did not translate, except I understood that she dreamed big and lost her dream. That was my Shaara.

# Thedar

I watched Tenor do the things that Shaarvan told him. I would have helped if he needed my assistance, but with Shaarvan giving directions, the ship seemed almost to land itself. Tenor identified the landing site, and the ship modified. Our descent was slow and steady, perfectly targeting a blank place on the Space Port.

I glanced over at Shaara. She looked practically immobile. Had the Power draw been too severe? Should we be worried? I checked with Spelon and Tura, aware that Shaarac was listening.

"Is she okay?" I asked. "Shaara," I said before they could speak.

"She has gone into shock," Tura said. "It was not from her use of Power. I checked her. She has tapped very little of it."

"Shock?" And then I understood. It was Shaarvan who had thrown her into this catatonic state. The poor kid was terrified.

"Spelon, take her to your room and choose an Altarian dress, one suitable for the wife of a lord. Shaara would hate us if we took her from the ship when she was not looking her best."

"Yes," he said, but I could tell he was almost as bad off as Shaara. Two with catatonia, I thought to myself. I removed Thaandar from his arms. The baby was sound asleep, unaware of the drama that was sure to come. Lucky baby.

Spelon stood up. I pulled him close to whisper in his ear. "We do what is best for Shaara always. Remember that."

Spelon nodded. "You are right, Thedar. I agree. An Altarian dress, one suitable for the wife of a noble."

I watched the two of them head back to their quarters, and then I looked down at Shaarac. The boy's eyes were full of excitement. He was fidgety and making a mess of the cookie he'd been given. I took a cloth and cleaned him up. The cookie was only crumbs. His clothes would still be adequate for greeting his father. I knew I should have put the boy into proper Altarian costuming, too, but someone needed to keep their eye on Tura. We still had suspicions about her.

"Come, Shaarac," I said. "Let's watch the landing. We are almost on Altar."

I juggled the baby so I could hold him one-handed. That allowed Shaarac to slip his small hand into mine. I was surprised to find it shaking.

So this was just as big an occasion for the child as it was for the mother. I think we often forgot that Shaarac had feelings just as intense as an adult. I would make sure that Shaarvan formally greeted the boy. His son needed that.

# Tura

The moment was almost here. The big event. I would meet the Shapechanger General. I had been instructed to kill him at the moment of my introduction. My Commoner sister had pleaded with me to do so, yet I hadn't decided yet if I should, which is why Tem, Tessa, and

Spelon, in their moments of intense study, could not read such an aim. But juggling secrets while in the passionate embraces of the two Shapechanger lords had been quite the challenge. An interesting one that even heightened the stimulation of our dalliances. But now, soon, I must choose. What would it be?

Getting to know Shaara had been remarkable. She really was as powerful as Tessa had told me. But there was more to the child than that. She was the sweetness long removed from the rest of us. We Priestesses had once upon time been more or less like Shaara, but males had robbed us of that joy, that innocence, that pureness of spirit.

A few times, Shaara had hinted at her degradation on Freinana, owned by a Commoner, beaten and bruised. Yet, she was still true to the essence of her that unique wholesomeness that seemed hers alone. She was utterly open, her thoughts a panorama of integrity. Had I ever been that genuine, that untouched by a universe of turpitude?

This Shaarvan, the one I was about to meet, had dragged her through Shapechanger training. That in itself had stripped many females from any semblance of peace. Even past the death of their husbands, they still writhed in their nightmares and burned with hatred for that past. Yet, Shaara loved him wholeheartedly. Even with Spelon, that heartthrob of a Shapechanger, at her side, his caring and commitment to her, an open admission that he loved her, she remained true to her husband.

I think she had earned her position among them. She hadn't waved her beauty in the faces of her guardians, parading it like some kind of trophy that allowed her to score unending victories over their devotion. She was kind to all of them, as loving as a child, and they were all infatuated with her. I had observed Tenor and Thedar. They kept her compartmentalized as their child, their ward, even as a daughter. Shaara could have enjoyed all their services during the many Passes they'd lived together in this pseudo-family they'd formed, but that wasn't her nature.

I hated her for that, yet I admired her. Such a bi-current of mixed feelings.

I could never join her crowd of devotees. I didn't have that in me, but if I ever allowed myself a friend, I would name her one. Or, at least, I'd aspire to become one.

But now the crossroad had reared its ugly head, and I must choose. A sister who I spent the first eighteen years of life with — she was older than me, a Commoner who had gone her way without a backward glance — or the new additions to my harem, the deliciousness of Spelon, and . . .

Steva, that was my sister's Altarian name. She had been bought by a wealthy Commoner. The details of her life still remained obscure. She hadn't told me all except that he, although not cruel, had certainly not been gentle. I think, reading between the lines, that she had poisoned him when he bought another woman, claiming that woman was to become Steva's new servant but appraising her with the eyes of one who hungered for more than the girl's ability to perform chores.

The ship touched down on the landing site gently, then rebalanced itself on the platform. Steam rolled out the sides, or what looked like steam. Thedar had said to expect a platoon of soldiers. I could see them surrounding a landing party, which I assumed included the questionable and renown Shaarvan.

The odds of my doing this deed that Steva had requested were less sure than I'd imagined, and for the first time, I realized that the result she envisioned would probably bring about my death. Was I willing to give my life for her cause? No.

And with that realization, the decision had been made. There might be other Tides for administering Shaarvan's one-way ticket into the other dimension, but it would not take place at our first meeting.

As the ship cooled down, its steam becoming less, Shaara and Spelon reentered the main room, and we prepared for our exit onto the planet. Shaara looked pale and sickly. Stress would do that even for the strong. But despite her faded appearance, she now looked ethereally magnificent, an even more delicate version of herself,

Long ago, but in my younger Tides, for a while the Shapechanger had captured women from a planet called Castorite. Those females were luminescent in the same manner as Shaara looked now. The Castorites had been very popular. Their beauty was impressive and desired by all. But they'd died, every one of them. Castorites, it seemed, could not live outside the realm of their world, and no amount of medical research could find the missing elements.

Shaara was not a Castorite, but perhaps her life would be equally limited. If I murdered her husband, that would be true. As a Saberey bondmate, she would die without her mate. I did not want to do that to her, to kill what was good and precious.

Tessa had told me in the strictest confidence that Shaara would, at some future date, become the Chief High Priestess, replacing herself in old age. Although foreseeing could fall apart when some great travesty of justice wiped out its base, I didn't long to be the Future's breakdown. Besides, I would like to see Shaara in that position. The gossip crones would lose their dominance, and the Institute might become the haven for women that it was meant to be. Perhaps I would even join then . . .

What was I thinking? I could never fit in. I laughed, not out loud, of course. The Shapechanger males were too tightly strung with nerves, all of them reflecting their princess' emotional distress.

Currently, with their bodies in rigid postures with stern facial muscles and tight grips on whatever they were holding, they had gone into pure Warrior mode. Any sharp moves on my part, or even a cackle like Tessa's, might set their pipes or cat shapes into action.

I fell in line for the exit from our ship. First came Shaara and Spelon. It was easy to see the connection between them. His body leaned into her. An experienced reader of such body signals, I could see that it was not that of a Shapechanger Lord, proclaiming the female as his. This was merely a protective stance. Spelon was showing the waiting party that no one could harm Shaara as long as he lived.

Tenor followed them, holding the baby. I was next. Then, practically stepping on my heels he rode me so closely, walked Tenor, his hand firmly attached to young Shaarac. Tenor's forceful push from behind threatened subtly. In spite of my decision not to reck havoc on this reunion, it was obvious I would be well-chaperoned, firmly squelched into a minor role, or none at all.

When I'd boarded the ship, I'd first thought that I could win over the girl's guardians, plying sex for allegiance, but neither Tenor nor Thedar had taken a step off their guardian podium. If there had been some kind of scale of loyalty, I would be down at the bottom, kick-worthy and alone. They were all firmly in the Shaara camp, no matter how many nights (and Tides) of sexual play we'd engaged in.

It had impressed me during our fiveTide together, observing the males with the children. Bottle-feeding and diaper changing, on hands and knees with the little one, while romping and tossing balls with the older and instructing him in the lore and etiquette of the Shapechanger. The lucky boys had been generously given three fathers and would soon know another.

I could not fault these Shapechanger Warriors in fidelity to their little family or in their behavior to me or with Shaara. They were a new breed. I wondered if Shaara would sway others towards this pattern. If the Commoners got their way, would she become Queen of Altar and change the whole framework of the Shapechanger?

Once I would have thought such a thing an impossibility.

No, there would be no deaths. I wanted to see how a future with someone like Shaara would unwind. Too many lives depended on it. Shaara could be the hope for the females all over Westla, Altar, and the other planets in the Shapechanger world. The truth of it is that I believed in her. Perhaps I was a member of the Shaara Camp, after all.

# *Chapter Thirteen*

## Shaarvan

In the battle of Chustan, a knife had pierced my arm. The blood had dripped freely, so there was no serious harm to my body, but the pain had been formidable, deep in the muscle region. My cry of agony had been silenced before it ever made its way into the cacophony of noise all around me.

No one knew of the injury except my mother, for she often tapped into my mind. (I had guarded well such things from my soulmate, Shaara. She believed that our battles were still only of the mind. I preferred her innocence in that respect.)

But the memory of that pain, the knife handle still dangling from muscle, the almost scream of pain, the worry that I might be too injured to hold my place in line — all that and more cascaded into my body when I saw her walking down the ramp. The pain was the same. No, that was not true. The pain of seeing Shaara was much more than a mere wounded arm.

For a moment I was transported to the Tide when I had first brought Shaara to Altar. I had been so rough with her back then. My body had fought hard to resist the magic of transformation, to be no longer alone, to be distanced from others. To mingle my soul in that way felt like an outreach of great privation, at least it had seemed so back then.

But those were mere excuses for the hardships I had foisted on her. As Mother would have put it, "I tortured Shaara with my rock-hard beliefs that gave no tenderness or understanding."

And now I was seeing her again, pale and trembling, still the young girl of Passes ago, but not. Ah, agony. How could I have compared a mere wound in the arm to this moment of torment? But I must continue to deny myself and remain the anchor of sternness. I had no choice but to send her away. Again.

Spelon walked as always at her side, a faithful friend, the Shapechanger Warrior I had placed second as her husband, behind Thal, who'd betrayed us all. Spelon had proven his worth.

Why had the Guardians brought Shaara with them? What cruelty to punish both Shaara and me a second time.

"Welcome. Altar blesses you this Tide," I said, welcoming them properly.

I saw myself then in my father's formality. Simple rituals often paused painful thoughts. Such subtle delays with the etiquette of cordiality were potent coverings for emotional distress. Ceremony invited new beginnings as if such were open to us now.

Yet, these guardians had served me well. They deserved no less. They had brought my sons here, even if unasked and unwanted, since the dangers were not past.

But I didn't plunge first into accusations as to why they'd come. I rested on ceremony. I introduced my mother to Thedar and Tenor, then gave my attentions to Shaarac. The boy had grown, of course. He was in a quandary as to whether to be shy with me or to run into my arms. I settled the issue and embraced him, leaving formality behind. He was enthusiastic for my attention then. He gushed most unshapechanger-like, but I smiled down in his face and welcomed his childlike babble.

Next, I greeted the baby in Thedar's arms. Thaandar, did they still call him that? I had not officially changed his name. I must make sure I quickly renamed him. Shaandar he would become since Thal had passed into the other realm. Shaandar was mine alone now. My second son.

I presented them both to my mother. Her eyes were full of delight. She hugged and kissed my sons, her grandchildren. She had known Shaarac only as a baby. He would have no recollection of her. It was with sadness that I realized that. I had cheated her (and myself) out of Passes of Shaarac's childhood.

And then the easy part had been dwelt with, and I must take up the hard. I greeted Spelon with all the respect he'd well earned. I thanked him for his care of Shaara. I acknowledged his position as a Second Husband. His eyes remained sheltered from me. Only his jawline hardened with tension, letting me know that he still waited for the judgment to come. I must allay his stress, but that would mean turning to her.

I inhaled my breath and glanced at her again. I had been wrong. The knife in my muscled arm was no more than a pin prick compared to what I saw in her eyes — the depths of anguish, the horror because she had already read my decision, the tears, unshed but felt so deeply it was if the Sabereys were once more shredding my skin with their claws.

"You should not have come," I told her, scorning the polite bandages of convention. For what was the point when we were as open to each other as if we stared into a mirror and saw ourselves. *Shaara, my soul, my love.*

"But you told us to come," she said, her voice so soft I almost didn't hear it, but, in our closeness, my mind had lost the ability to shut her out.

"What?" A flash of understanding seared me. A sudden search of the platform said we still had a moment to spare.

"Quickly," I shouted. "We must go at once."

But it was already too late. We had dallied too long in our greetings. I called the soldiers to arms, alerted Shaara's guardians, and corralled the children and females. Who was the stranger? My mind asked, taking note of a female's presence. A Priestess my Power informed me. Later, I would analyze that. Not now when every moment was essential for the protection of my loved ones.

The Commoners had miscalculated. They had not sent sufficient numbers to overpower my troops. They realized it a short time later after half of them lay dying on the pathways of Space Port. My platoon was better armed and prepared.

The Shapechanger Warriors quickly turned their mindpower on the Commoners, many of whom suddenly aimed weapons at each other, lost in an assault of Mind Force they couldn't fight. Then, confusion cost the remaining attackers.

Those who still could fled, retreating at a run. We did not chase them. Many of my platoon laughed. I did not encourage that, but I said nothing to dissuade them. Victory should be celebrated.

But my poor Shaara, always sheltered from such strife, was glassy-eyed from shock. I could not ascertain if seeing the deaths of so many was the root of her dismay or if the treachery of my rejection had caused her devastation. I supposed it did not matter.

My mother, the children, the guardians, and the unknown Priestess were all uninjured. We had been fortunate since there had been no time to take real cover and no place to hunker down.

I didn't want to invite Shaara back to my parent's house, but the battle action had forced my hand. She was not safe here, out in the open. I knew she would not leave her children without a fight nor retreat back to the ship, having come this far. Besides, my mother would not permit such an abrupt cleaving. She would want to exchange words with Shaara and share memories, as females did. And Shaara would want to see Tevor, that I knew.

I glanced at the stray Priestess and nodded my head, not a proper greeting, but the only one I would take the time to make. I hustled us all forward. The private car I'd arranged for, instead of public transport, would race us home. It was not an Altarian socially acceptable practice, but needs must come before the Altaian code of behavior. Besides there were not as many conveyances anymore, the war having disrupted many such services.

We were crammed into the pilotcar. I removed the current pilot and took over the pilot's seat. Teea sat in Thedar's lap, the Priestess on Tenor's, and Shaara took Spelon's lap, a fact which disturbed my inner calm. The baby was held by Shaara and my mother held Shaarac. We were cramped, but the war had taught me many things. Such deprivations were the least of my problems.

# Teea

I had much to tell Shaara. I was glad that circumstance had forced Shaarvan to bend against his personal wishes and allow my daughter to return to the house with us.

Yes, I could tell that he had crushed her again with the sharpness of another dismissal, but did she understand his reasons? Did she see that he was afraid for her life? Did she know that he still loved her?

I could not talk with her here in a crowded pilot car. Shaarvan would command me to silence. I could not risk that, although as the war continued, there was far less dominance in Shapechanger males. It was as if their eyes had opened to see females carrying weapons in their hands and floods of widows fighting for Altar, as well as their own rights. Traditions on Altar were changing. Some of it was good.

But Shaarvan, although he realized that the past authority and control of males was slipping away, was still irresolute in his values. During his long search for Shaara, I thought his opinions about the slave trade had been altered, maybe even softened to some extent, but then the war had arrived and later Shaara's Priesthood candidacy, which had halted his self-examinations. Now, I no longer knew my son. He was once again an impassive, inscrutable stranger.

I pushed thoughts of that away to converse with my grandson. What a joy it was to finally meet him as more than a baby. He could talk now, which he seemed to like to do. He told me all about his mother's landoor on Westla and the chair named Stuba he rode. I gathered the chair was also a landoor.

Oh, dear, that might cause complications with Tren's gift, I thought, but then I became lost in Shaarac's chatter about an animal called a podo who chased sticks. How one could chase a stick, I didn't quite understand, but if the podo was anything like an Earth dog, I supposed that chasing them was more like retrieving them. In that sense, I was able to follow.

Except while I was remembering dogs, Shaarac had skipped to talking about the Westlan zoo and how they had an animal that sounded like a turtle, based on Shaarac's description, but that wore a smile on its face. I wondered if it were a real animal or just a robotic one.

Then there were the fish who would come up to get the food he threw. That tale pinged Earth memories as well. I smiled down at my grandson, wishing I had something exciting to offer about Altar, but I couldn't think of anything that could rivel zoo animals or stick-chasing podos.

My legs were cramping by the time we reached the house. I wouldn't have traded such an inconvenience for anything. though. I had a grandson — no, two of them. I glanced over at Shaara's armful of wiggling baby. Thaandar was at a delightful stage, full of giggles. I wanted to press my nose into his belly and blow funny noises at him. That had always sent my young ones into fits of laughter.

At the house, I waited my turn to crawl out of the vehicle. It shouldn't be that painful, but my bones didn't agree. The Shapechanger who'd been Shaara's seat, Spelon, I think he was called, helped me out. Such a handsome one. He had a jawline that practically urged to be petted. I bet Shaara agreed with me. She seemed very close with her Second Husband.

Such strange customs Shapechanger had, I thought for the thousandth time. I supposed the other two guardians with Shaara were number three and four. Both were handsome Warriors and seemingly dedicated to her as much as Spelon obviously was, yet her eyes were fastened on Shaarvan. She was drinking in the sight of him as I did with Tevor.

The woman — Shaarvan had called her a Priestess — introduced herself to me. She said she was a medic who Tem had sent to offer up a second opinion about Tevor's condition. Did I dare hope? My heart sped up, adrenaline showering me with anticipation for a miracle cure.

I would have peppered Tura with questions if I'd had the opportunity, but Shaarvan was already pushing us forward, his eyes doing a danger survey. The house was well guarded. Military troops surrounded us, along with a new high-powered fence that would shock anyone without the special code.

But Shaarvan never trusted anyone now. Thenos had been the cause of that. When Shaarvan found out from Tem that the pre-school that Shaarac had attended had been bombed, Shaarvan paced the house in desperation. He'd almost flown to Westla himself to storm the paths of West, hunting for the villain. He'd also debated storming into Thenos' palace to attack the brother responsible for it.

Starnkor, my Second, had talked him out of both reprisals, saying there were other ways to revenge ourselves against Thenos. But all the efforts of the Shapechanger hadn't done what Shaara did. She ended it. There would be no more bombing children, no more schemes to steal Shaara for his own purposes. Shaara had decided to end the war and get her husband back. Who could blame her? Except for her Shapechanger husband.

Shaarvan thought his sacrifice to give her freedom was a reward. But I think his feelings had merely been hurt because she had done what he couldn't. A girl he'd raised to be his wife with all the trainings and even the torture of Saberey claws had still disobeyed his order.

She had killed the monster, the one he was supposed to bring down. How that must hurt his ego!

But laying my bitterness aside, I entered the house then rushed immediately to Tevor. My dear husband, my soulmate, lay as he'd done for several Passes, no better or worse. The poisons of Thenos, we all believed, were at the root of it. But Parthrol, the only one who might have known a curative, the anti-venom to the drug, was dead. Thenos, it was believed, was the one who had blown up the moon where Parthrol lived.

I sat down beside Tevor, picked up his hand, and told him about Shaara's arrival. I never knew if my husband could hear anything I said, but I felt closer to him when I spoke. It was almost like having him back.

Starnkor, my Second, walked in after a few moments.

"I placed the guests in rooms. You should have done that, Teea."

He was gentle with his scold. I knew he was right, but instinct had driven me to sit with Tevor to tell him that Shaara was here. I signed the gesture of contrition, and Starnkor accepted it.

"Come," he said. The Priestess medic must be introduced to Tevor. Then you will know if there is hope."

He placed his hand on my arm. I could not object. I had more to tell Tevor, but it would have to wait. I was not a Priestess as Shaara was. I must obey my Second.

# Tura

I had little hope for Tevor. Seeing him in person with no signs of consciousness, no reaction in his pupils to the light I shone into them, no reflexes, no reaction to any stimulus — it seemed pretty clear that his body was no more than a cask of the former Shapechanger. But I offered a whisp of promise to his wife.

"We will try this medication from the Institute," I said, pulling out the ampoule that Tessa had given me. I used an eyedropper to inject single drops of the liquid into her husband's mouth. There must be some small awareness left in his body. As the drops slowly entered his throat, he swallowed. When the vial was completely empty, having poured the last droplets into his mouth, I recapped the bottle and stepped away.

It was only then that I realized that Shaara was standing in the doorway. "May I come in?" she asked.

I nodded, then looked to Teea. She reached out her hand and took Shaara's. "Speak to him, Shaara. Maybe he will hear you."

I examined Tevor one last time, then shook my head. The dose given to him should have had an immediate effect. But it didn't. I had no other miracles to offer. Tevor was gone. But I did not say that to his wife. I left the two of them to talk to the Shapechanger, who had already ventured into another realm.

Starnkor, a very handsome Shapechanger, led me to my room. I thought about inviting him to share it with me, but this was Altar. They were known to be prudish in such matters. It would be better to wait for his departure and then find Thedar or Tenor. Unfortunately, neither of them were in their assigned rooms.

As I searched the house, I ran into another gorgeous male — absolutely one of my favorite types. He was the kind who carried a hint of danger in his aura. I knew in an instant that he would fit my bedroom style perfectly.

I lay on the charm, gave him my wide-eyed damsel in distress look, the seductress peering up at him under slinky lashes, and the saucy, head-tossing wench. Not one of my personas was successful. The Shapechanger eyed me with politely veiled scorn. "And you are?" he asked.

I thought I had him then. Most males trembled slightly at the word Priestess, but sadly, this one did not.

"Did you find her, Tren?" Thedar asked, interrupting all my efforts to imprint the dashing male.

Since I was standing in front of Thedar, and he didn't have the look of one who had found someone he was looking for, I surmised that the *she* they were discussing was Shaara. Not another spellbound hunk of malehood, I wanted to cry out in jealousy. How did such a quiet, thoughtful girl create such a huge gathering of delectables? It wasn't fair.

I had long ago transformed myself into a younger model, one with shiny hair down to my bottom, slightly curled, slightly tousled. My face was unlined and smooth with just the faintest of touchups, the kind that perked a male's interest. I had seen myself in the mirror. I could compete quite nicely with dainty little Shaara. And I had *boobs*.

Yet Tren, although fully aware of my seductive moves, had shown absolutely no interest. Once Thedar arrived, he probably forgot he'd asked me my name, or had he? "I'm Tura," I told him, hoping he'd ask where I'd come from what I was doing there.

Instead, he ignored me and turned back to Thedar. "So where is she?"

I sighed, seeing that this was getting me nowhere. This gorgeous Shapechanger didn't seem to be aware that I was still standing there, tapping my foot with impatience.

"If you're looking for Shaara. She is with Teea. They were both in the room with Tevor — at least they were there when I left.

I knew the moment it rolled off my tongue that I'd said the wrong thing. Mentioning Shaara had wiped his mind of me. Nothing to do to patch it up. I turned an about-face and returned to my room.

# Tren

I knew a cold one when I met one. This female was the worst kind. I could sense she would entertain a male in bed with a high-energy romp if he were willing to take a *Chingong* as a bed partner. But *Chingongs* were vicious predators that would devour you after churning your guts into sour porridge. I knew the kind of plays that female would hand out. She'd take pleasure in twisting a male's insides into ropes, then expect him to beg on his knees until she allowed him a second chance. No thanks.

Besides Shaara was here, and I hadn't said my hellos. The urgency in me multiplied, yet I needed to know first how Shaarvan had treated her. "Did he accept her back?"

"No," Thedar said, his eyes darkening with fresh sadness. "At the Space Port, his thoughts, whatever they were, practically slapped her in the face. He demanded to know why she had arrived like he had not been the one to send for us. I do not understand. If he did not want her on Altar, why did he tell her to come?"

"I doubt he sent anything to Westla. We have been in a blackout for a twentyTide. No ships out, no messages through spacetime sendings. And you say he wrote her?"

Thedar's expression, usually adroitly expressionless, now wrinkled with puzzlement. "Tem got a short letter, more like a note. Shaarvan spoke of Tevor, of the battles being fewer, and of Teea needing Shaara's company. He wanted his children. It was sparse and unfeeling. Its coldness hurt our girl. But she was still eager to come. We could not have left her there or stolen her children from her. Shaarvan is wrong in his plans for her. He crushes her heart with his cruelty."

"You think I hurt her intentionally? Have you not heard there is a war going on?" Shaarvan growled, approaching us from behind.

"First off, you need to know that you were duped," Shaarvan said. "I did not write you to come. I would not have wished to endanger any of you."

"I told him you did not write that note, but it is obvious their purpose in sending it," I said. "They will try to kidnap Shaara and Thaandar."

"Shaandar," Shaarvan corrected. "His name is to be recorded as Shaandar."

The hallway was getting crowded. We heard Shaara and Teea walking towards us. Their voices were low and sad. It was obvious they were discussing Tevor.

"Come," Shaarvan ordered, "There is much to discuss. We must gather Tenor and Spelon and find an unused room to talk."

He turned, expecting us to follow. It was obvious he wished to avoid Shaara. I was surprised that he'd revert to dodging and hiding. Wasn't that very unShapechanger-like?

"Then we must include Teea and Shaara, for it concerns them, too," Thedar told him, asserting his wishes, and also, I think, indicating that Shaarvan's actions were disappointing.

Shaarvan turned back to glare at Thedar. "Things have changed that much?" my brother asked, raising an eyebrow in disbelief.

The females had caught up with us. Shaara's eyes immediately went to Shaarvan, drinking him in, building memories, I presumed.

He didn't look at her or greet her. I thought about what Thedar had said. I felt like punching my brother in the nose. It would serve him right.

"Shaara," I said softly.

She looked up at me and ran into my arms. "Tren," she said, "Oh, Tren." She burst into tears, wetting my shirt as she had so often done on Freinana.

Feelings I couldn't allow swept over me. I hugged her tightly, but inside my head, I was reminding myself that she was not mine and could never be mine. She was now my sister. I must treat her as such.

But for the moment, all I could do was hold her and let her tears wash away the grief until it suddenly hit me that the Shapechanger standing there were probably all about to rend my skin into strips.

"Shaara," I said, trying to push her away. "Shaara, they will not allow this. I do not want to see you punished again, my little sister."

Finally, she looked up at me, her deep, gray eyes awash with tears. "Who would care?" she asked bitterly. "My husband?" She snorted, issuing a laugh so bitter and anguished it sounded nothing like the sweet girl I'd known in Freinana. What had they done to her?

I looked up at my brother. Shaarvan's face was not as expressionless as the one he usually showed the world. His eyes looked haunted, like a man fragmented by what he could not have. I saw no anger, though, only a dull-eyed resignation.

Thedar's eyes were boring into mine. He was shaking his head. I could interpret his meaning. He was warning me that I was playing with explosives. From whom? Shaarvan or Spelon?

And then I heard the roar of a Saberey. Spelon had arrived, his face in half-change, his eyes green with animosity.

"Shaara," I warned.

She sensed him, too. She held her hand up, and I saw a man clothed in black in some kind of officer's uniform, standing at a crosswalk, directing vehicles. I read the notion in her mind, although I had no idea what it meant.

Apparently, either the image or her spread-open vertical hand paused Spelon's onward rush. He reappraised the situation, shot a glance at Shaarvan, then at Thedar. To my astonishment, the Shapechanger's face changed, his dark patterns sliding back into smooth planes with skin. The flaring green eyes turned back to gray.

"Shaara," was all he said.

She turned from me, then threw herself at Spelon. "It's too much," she said. "I thought I could take it. But I can't."

I think it was obvious then. All eyes turned to Shaarvan. He didn't roar as Spelon had done, but the urge to do so was evident. He once had been our leader, but now he was the villain. I could read that appraisal from every person in the group.

Tenor had joined us, adding the brunt of his animosity to the rest of the group. Only Teea hung back, caught between the son she loved and the Shapechanger who tortured her daughter. In her eyes, I saw doubt almost as big as the ship we'd come in.

Thedar, always the wise one, broke in. "We were just about to head to a place where we could all sit down and discuss the situation. Teea, can you suggest a neutral spot?"

And so, as if the past moment had not occurred, we moved as a group toward the table near the food machines. It was a large-sized one with sufficient chairs for all.

"Where are the boys?" Shaara asked, rousing herself to look about as if she expected to see the children playing nearby.

Teea answered quickly. "They are with the servant girl, Neda. She is not Shapechanger, Shaara, but she was a slave to a good man who died in a battle. We took her in. She told me that she would be happy to play babysitter to your children."

"And you trust her?" Shaara asked before one of her guardians could speak.

"The children are content. I just checked on them," Tenor said.

Starnkor wandered in. "May I join you?" he asked.

I gave introductions to those who had not yet met him. When I told them he was Teea's Second, Shaara bolted up. "No, not you, too," she said.

Shapechanger customs were still new to me, but I understood now about the biologically programmed needs of the females. Starnkor's presence as Teea's Second had not been a frivolous decision on

Tevor's part. I had discussed it with Pathe, Shaarvan's medically trained brother (and now mine, when I remembered it since Shaarvan had forced me into the Trendacons family with my transition.)

It seems that female Shapechanger must engage with a male, or they became crazed and locked into a Saberey change. After too much time without a male, the female would no longer be able to change back to her two-legged form.

The original Shapechanger programmers had much to be blamed for, including the scarcity of women since their gene manipulations destroyed female embryos. But since the programmers were all dead, no one could hold them accountable for their numerous mistakes.

Starnkor was watching Shaara rather nervously it seemed. "You are a Priestess," he said, bowing his head to her.

With his sign of respect, Shaara swallowed her rage, nodded the barest greeting, then slipped back into her chair. She did not look up, possibly afraid to glance at Teea. Spelon took her hand and drew it into his lap.

My head swung to Shaarvan. His eyes had followed the action and were frozen on the sight of their shared hands. His face had paled. His cheekbones were flexed with tension.

So, my brother was not as cold to his wife as he pretended to be. I noted it, then scanned the others.

"After our discussion, Shaara, I would like to show you something outside," I said.

If I'd thought Shaarvan's cheekbones were twitching with the sight of twined hands, I was amazed to see how much reaction his face displayed with my mention of the something I had to show Shaara.

My present to her had been the source of one of our greatest fights. Only Starnkor's level-headedness had stopped Shaarvan and me from turning violent. But Shaarvan was still not letting it go. My gift to his wife continued to rile him beyond measure.

Too bad. He must deal with it. And with her.

Meanwhile, Spelon was now glaring at me, misunderstanding my words. "You are invited to see what I have to show her," I told Spelon, nodding respectfully to show I recognized his relationship with Shaara and did not mean this as a threat to his connection.

He seemed appeased then. Shaara appeared intrigued. She fostered a hint of a smile, which, under the circumstances, felt like a vast improvement to her mood.

But I had stolen Tenor's attention away from business. I flashed a gesture of contrition, the modified version used only by males.

"Okay, first, is it true that you did not send the note to Tem telling us to fly to Altar?" Tenor asked.

"I did not send it," Shaarvan said, gritting his teeth. "I would not have risked any of you that way,"

Was he talking about his children, or did that include Shaara, I wondered. Did he care enough to worry about her safety?

"So we have arrived prematurely," Tenor continued, but we are here now, so we must make the best of it. You will be able to get to know your sons, Shaarvan. I assume we will be safe inside this fenced and guarded area?"

Shaarvan nodded but still looked worried. "Yes, but you have brought the jewels into proximity. Every Commoner will be on alert for a way to steal Shaandar and Shaara from our protection. They will do everything to achieve that aim."

I wasn't sure what the guardians and Shaara knew. I figured it was time to fill in the spaces. "They believe Shaara to be the Queen of Altar. Her son, Shaandar, whom they call Thenon, is the royal heir. Strange, I know. Little Shaara was once only a mere slave on Freinana."

Apparently, such knowledge was supposed to be suppressed. The indrawn breath at the table let me know that I had just treaded on a field mine.

But then Shaara laughed. "I missed you, Tren," she said. "Have you started building another casino yet?"

Her small white teeth flashed in a manner that sent a pang to my stomach. Funny way to put it, like love, had anything to do with hunger pains. I steadied my expressions, alert to the fact that I was sitting at a table with Shapechanger, who could dig secrets from the depths of your soul. Oh, well, mine were readily available. I had hid nothing from Shaarvan.

"Shaara, we were discussing the situation. Please, stay on task," Tenor said gently.

Shaarvan snorted. "Like that is a possibility."

With his words, the tension mounted again. Perhaps we should just put up a boxing ring and allow everyone to slug it out. But then I saw the hurt in Shaara's eyes, the fresh pain. I remembered then that a boxing ring would not solve this state of affairs, although a few jabs at Shaarvan might make us all feel better.

The discussion about what to do went on and on with no solutions. At last, I interrupted again and said, "I'm taking Shaara outside to see the trees."

"Trees?" she cried out. "I don't remember any trees here."

Once more, Shaarvan made a disconcerting noise, one of disgust perhaps? I ignored him, stood up, and watched to see if Shaara (and Spelon) would follow. I was not disappointed. Everyone joined in, following me out to the backyard where the present I'd purchased for Shaara was waiting.

The grasslands spread out for a large expanse. It was now fenced in, and I'd planted trees that had grown some but were far shorter than I wished. But the trees were not really the reason I'd brought Shaara outside.

A sharp neigh split the air, then a moving force of black muscle, hooves, and a majestic head of a bugled warning approached at full gallop. I turned from the sight to watch Shaara's face. I was not disappointed.

It was like a plate full of sprila cookies to a young child, a pile of gold to an avaricious Commoner, a pile of chips to a gambler. Shaara's face was lit up with a joy so immense it was spellbinding.

But that was only a moment's sight because the next, she was running full blast to the fence, sobbing with happiness. "Crimson Black. My sweet, sweet landoor. Crimson!"

She climbed that fence faster than a male could have, her dress flashing trim legs in a manner most unseemly, at least by Altar's prudish standards. But I had seen more of her that first time, stretched out on the bed of her former master, and then later, just after she'd stripped for a dive into cool lake water.

Of those who stood beside me, only Teea and Starnkor gasped, probably not from the show of Shaara's gorgeous legs or her unstructured abandonment of protocol but from her daring. For the stallion was rearing and cavorting in elation at this reunion. His throat was issuing nickers of excitement and familiarity. He was prancing and kicking his hind hooves, careful not to harm Shaara.

190

It was at that moment I realized the beast was sentient and aware of the fragility of the girl. And it was obvious to me that he loved her as much as I did. I hadn't realized a landoor could have such deep feelings. Despite my brother's ire at my purchase and transport of the landoor, I knew I had done the right thing. This was meant to be.

The landoor had calmed and was nuzzling Shaara's hair, his nostrils blowing huge puffs of horse breath at her. Shaara was hugging him as if he were a small stuffed doll she slept with. It was an unbelievable sight.

"I think Mandar has been replaced," Thedar said.

It was a strange, incomprehensible comment. I glanced his way only a moment, then returned to watching Shaara and her landoor.

"I have never seen Shaara this happy before," Teea said.

"Of course not. She was with me before. Is that what you're saying. How I mishandled her and brutalized her daily?"

Shaarvan didn't wait for his mother's response but stormed off in a sea of jealousy, guilt, and anger. The haze of yellow and its pungency followed him back into the house.

"Shaara is not the only one hurting," Spelon said, surprising me because I'd never noticed him being all that empathetic.

Although my eyes wanted to watch Shaara with her beloved Crimson, I couldn't help surveying her three guardians. "None of you look alarmed by the landoor. Have you seen one before?"

Spelon grunted. "We have spent considerable time at a landoor ranch. We are familiar with the smelly beasts."

"We bought her a landoor. Mandar is still on Westla. I don't know what will happen to him if we stay here. Would two landoors fight each other if we managed to fly him here as you did?" Thedar asked, his eyes still watchful of Shaara and the unknown landoor. "I thought Mandar was risky, but this landoor looks even more dangerous," he added.

"She can handle him," I said. "He was a wild beast, unrideable, before she started working with him. His former owner said he could have been a champion jumper, but he will not work with any of the trainers. Blaire said that he is a one-person landoor."

"She does have the ability to charm the savage beast," Teea said musingly.

I glanced at Shaarvan's mother. She was still watching Shaara, but I wondered if she was only talking about landoors.

# Shaara

I knew I should immediately have turned around and thanked Tren. I couldn't imagine how much it had cost to buy Crimson Black, a top show landoor, and then to have him shipped all the way to Altar. How could a person do that? Did they put him into a deep sleep during transit? How had they transported him even onto the ship? He was difficult to work with, even for experienced landoor grooms.

But, although a part of me said I should thank Tren this very moment, the stronger part of me said that it was more important to reaffirm my relationship with Crimson. We had been separated for so long. I was surprised he even knew me. But there was no question he did. His nickers and deep-seated rumbles of almost cat purrs, his breath blowing into my hair and the way he leaned into me, his head squeezing into my neck so he could better inhale my scent. Oh, he remembered me without a doubt.

I whispered to him how much I'd missed him, how the decision to leave him had not been mine but was forced upon me. Although when I sat atop him, it had always felt like we were one, I doubted he understood my words. For one thing, I'd been speaking in Altarian, not Freinanan, but did a landoor even relate to the babbling of any language?

Of course, he knew certain words. We'd drilled with walk, trot, canter, gallop. He understood the meaning of those words. Thinking about that, recollecting the joy of having put him through his paces, made me yearn to jump up on him and ride. But I had no trousers like the ones Spelon had given me or blue jean material like I'd worn on Freinana when everyone thought I was a boy.

But who can argue with a driving force? "Down," I ordered.

Crimson without needing any repetition, dropped to his knees and collapsed for me to climb on. My dress, with absolutely no buffer to prevent the rash of unprotected inner thighs, squished upwards as I sat down.

I heard Spelon yell out. Whether he was censoring my flash of naked flesh or warning me of the irritation against my skin, it didn't matter. Crimson and I were once again one. I leaned over whispered the word he was hoping to hear.

"Go," I said. Not a gated, refined movement fit for the show ring, this was a mostly forbidden okay to gallop to his delight. And we did. The wind whistled through my hair, tossing it like leaves in a storm. My face stung with the force of it. Crimson was fast, a ground-swallowing comet.

The fenced-in field was huge. We explored its vast interior, then when Crimson was heaving from lack of breath, I gentled him down with only my voice and seat, because I'd never even thought about finding a bridle. We walked an equal distance to our run, then slowly made our way back to where I'd left my family.

Someone had brought out chairs. Everyone was sitting, waiting for my return. All of them except Shaarvan. A stab of pain hit my chest, but it was less now. Crimson had taken away some of my agony. As if the thought had penetrated his brain, Crimson nickered softly.

I slipped off him on his opposite side, not wanting to invite inspection of my unclothed bottom half. My dress fell back, covering me once again. One more heavy embrace with my landoor soulmate, and then with a huge smile on my face, I turned, ready to face lectures and stern looks.

Surprisingly, there were few of them. Tura had joined the group. She wrinkled her nose as I approached.

"Pee-yew," she griped. "Someone needs a shower."

I laughed. All the joy in the universe was flowing in my veins. Nothing could bother me.

Spelon stood up and walked over to me. He kissed my nose and said, "I agree. Let's get you in that shower and salve the damage you have done,"

That was all the umbrage I received. There are times when miracles still occur.

# Shaarvan

So I made a scene, opening my sores for public viewing. I had nothing further to say. I might as well step out of the picture and leave her to absorb my current home and family. It would be equitable justice for all I had done to her.

With that thought, I made my way to Pathe's residence. He was treating a patient in the office when I arrived, his new wife at his side.

I sat down to wait, knowing I should not invade the female's privacy.

When she and her husband, a younger Shapechanger that I did not know well, Katron, I believed he was called, exited from their medical visit, we exchanged formal nods, and they sped by me a little quicker than one would expect for a pregnant wife, but then, perhaps they were rushing off for another appointment.

I doubted that, though. My presence often sent others speedily off. Was it my position in the new government, or as Pathe often told me, a reflection of my unpleasant gruffness?

Pathe waved me inside. His wife was no longer beside him. She and I had never become family. It was something I still needed to resolve. The fault was mine, of course. So far, I lacked not only the time for such matters, but the inclination.

"What brings you in my direction?" Pathe asked, studying me as he always did.

I hoped he found what he was looking for in my appearance or expression, but he did not comment. He turned to sterilize the instruments he had used with his patient.

I thought about the oddness of his question's phrasing. Was it accusatory? Pathe and I had not always gotten along. Our viewpoints were too different. Yet, he was friendly with Tren. They seemed to be melding nicely, so I assumed the fault was in me. I was feeling that defect a lot lately.

"A letter was sent to Tem on Westla." I began.

"Yes. I know where Tem lives. I am glad you wrote to him."

"I did not. It was not sent by me, but it requested Shaara's guardians to bring the children here. They arrived yesterTide."

"All of them?" Pathe said, staring at me more intently this time. "The guardians and Shaara?"

"Yes."

There was silence then. It gave me time to study the wall posters, the pictures of babies, and the diagram of a female's internal paraphernalia. Not things I wanted to look at, but better than Pathe's face.

"Have you welcomed her back? Are you reunited?"

I breathed in deeply and fought to regain my composure. "She is with Spelon. They said Stegthal, Thal as he last called himself, died. I do not know the details of that. They did not tell me."

"So another beds your wife. Is that not painful for you?"

The conversation was not going well. I decided to end it. "Bring your wife if you like and come visit at the house. You and she were fond of each other. I would think you might want to exchange pleasantries. And you can meet my two sons."

"I met Shaarac, as you recall. I was there."

"I must go. Tidings to your wife."

I walked out of Pathe's office even faster than Katron and his pregnant wife had trotted past me. It seemed that jogging was the new escape.

The soldiers surrounding me at my exit were, as always, on alert. We walked back to the private car I was using, the one I had commandeered more or less for my use during the war. It was not a moneyed vehicle. No shiny, polished chrome or racing strips on the tail fins, but it served its purpose. It got me where I need to go, only this time, it did not.

Although skilled mechanics kept it aligned and its parts in top condition, it failed to start. I opened the transot system and peered in, but that area was not in my expertise. Show me a spaceship, and I knew every component, but not on a private car. I'd previously never owned one.

Working on the principle that removing various components, checking for minute cracks, and then resetting the piece back into its place might fix the problem, kept me from being attentive to the dangers of wartime's marauding troops. Apparently, that was true for the soldiers who were standing guard as well.

The first time it registered on me that all was not well, I found myself surrounded by Commoners with pipes in their hands. Although I could have defended myself from four or five such men, there were too many to fight either with fists, Shapechange, or Mind Force. I raised my hands and surrendered.

As the "most wanted" on their list, I am sure they were thrilled to have caught me. I cursed myself for allowing my brain to be tumbled by stupidity and knotted up in the recall of my recent moments with Shaara. It was a fatal combination. Although, perhaps it was suitable for a Shapechanger with my personal darkness.

With one plunge of a knife, the Commoners could have ended the major burr in the last whimper of their rebellion. It could have solved the mess I'd made with my wife, too. A double positive.

But it quickly became obvious that the Commoners had no intention of giving me a speedy and easy goodbye. They took me to Thenos' palace and, for some reason, chained me to his throne.

Had I become a personal grievance of one of the rebels? Was I to become the revenge of his misfortunes?

Soldiers fed me, watered me, and then left me alone. That was the last thing I needed because then there was nothing I could do but wallow through past memories of my calamitous treatments of Shaara. It was a vile punishment they were inflicting on me. Deserved, maybe, but much more torturous than if they had merely opened a few veins, leaving me to decompose as a bloodless corpse.

I could see through the windows of the great hall I was in. Darkness was descending over Altar. It was the only way I had of knowing how much time had passed. I wondered if I'd have another night before moving on to the next realm. Was that a good thing?

Would I pay for the errors I had perpetuated in this domain on into the next? Was such punishment cumulative? Perhaps I kept adding piles of misdeeds until, at the end of the cycle, I was burdened so greatly with them that I sank down, buried by the rockslides of my transgressions.

When the night was full, the darkness only relieved by our remaining moon, I knew that my doom was to be slow torture. Perhaps they would feed me again, prolonging my life. How many Tides would I live, fastened to my brother's throne?

It had certainly not served him well. The throne he had built beside it was a smaller one, feminine. Had he designed it for Shaara? But Shaara would not have bent to his will. She would have died first. He never understood that.

Her Power had flared even before all the turmoil. She had almost perished in the snow when I had been too harsh with her. Had Thenos been unaware of her ability to choose death?

My parents had stopped her. Teea had told her about love. But what could Shaara possibly know about love? She'd received little of it from me. I'd crushed her with the Saberey scratches, and I'd criticized her, demoralized her, taken away her strengths, and, in general, beaten her down in every way possible until I'd robbed her of everything she'd been. I had taken away all her joy.

Yet, she still rose up out of the pain and despair to tell me she loved me. Why? How? She is an indomitable woman, unceasing in her loyalty, truth in the heart of corruption, endurance to the extreme. She was unique in every way, but I had failed to see it. So rigid was I with the rules of Altar, the dominance of the Shapechanger male, I had made every bad choice possible.

If I could have wept from the wrongs I had done to her, I would have. Perhaps in time, it would come to that. But, somewhere in the middle of my brewing over my Passes of cruelty, Commoners came to me, unfastened my chains, and escorted me to the necessary room. I was eager to relieve myself, but when I finished, I tried to find a way to escape. That was not allowed. Pain sticks hustled me back to my spot by the throne. The Commoners refastened me and left me again.

And so, of course, my thoughts drifted back to Shaara. She was everywhere I looked. And everything reminded me of her.

During the war, many Shapechanger females had offered themselves to me. It would have been easy to use them for a while, but I had lost my will to dip my flesh into another, to join my breath with theirs, to impart even that small part of me into one who was not my Shaara.

My thoughts were often hot with lust. A smile offered. A flash of breast hidden in cloth. A leg revealed, a voice that sounded like hers, hair the special color of hers, or the way an unknown female tossed her flowing hair over her shoulder. Shaara had been all around me even then — all around me, but not.

And then she traveled to me. Impossible. Only a seer was able to do that. A Priestess, perhaps. But an untrained wife? Teea had said it was love that gave Shaara that ability. My mother had said that it was only possible if I loved her that fiercely back. And I had. I did.

Love.

Everywhere, Shaara was loved. Is loved.

Except by me. Because now I am separate, dry as scattered leaves, desolate and broken. Pathe said it is only that I am closed off. He says that Shaara would open to me again and allow all that I yearn for to flow back inside me. But it is too late. I will die here, never having told her how I feel, never getting the chance to tell her how wrong I have been. The opportunity for it is gone now.

Thedar asked me on the ship if I felt hatred and bitterness for Thal, for his actions. How could I hate him, knowing that he yearned for what I had been given freely, what I had rejected. Bitterness was at the heart of both of us. He, because he could not possess her soul, and

I, because I had her soul but could no longer allow the wickedness that was inside me to possess her.

My body felt cramped in the position they had chained me in, but that ache was less than what I felt in my heart. The misery over what I had lost so needlessly, my Shaara, my love, plagued me. It should have kept me awake through all the hours of my self-induced torment, but with the sky as dark as an empty sky, sleep overcame my will.

I dreamed of her. Another form of punishment. She was smiling at me, her heart so full of love, it was a battering ram pounding into my soul. I felt her kisses on my cheek, on my forehead, then on my lips. I sank into her, a male deprived of sustenance for too long.

"I love you," she said in my dream, and in the dream, I answered her back, "I love you."

But dreams are only a combination of yearning and of wish fulfillment unless they are nightmares, stuck in the realm of trauma that life punishes you with. My pleasant dream proceeded to plunge over the ridge, falling into the latter.

It taunted me with scenes of Spelon in bed with her, pounding into Shaara as she moaned and quivered beneath him. They had only just finished that one last gasp of flight when Tren entered the room. He was carrying a whip and lashed downwards. Shaara cried out, begging for him to stop. Spelon's back split open. The blood flowed. The mighty warrior sank to the floor, and then there was only Tren and that whip.

I writhed from the heartache of seeing my love being beaten, but I was secured to Thenos' gold throne and could not get loose to protect her. As the agony grew fiercer, I woke.

I realized then that it was only a dream, a nightmare of my worries for Shaara.

Commoners again took me to the necessary room. Once more, I took care of my body's essentials. When the painsticks directed me back to the throne, fresh food and water sat there waiting for me.

A prisoner must always consider whether it is better to eat and drink to satisfy needs or to fast in order to die sooner. Something inside us makes that decision. Most of the time, we choose to linger even if the consequences are a slower death. I chose that, hope still inside me that I might somehow free myself from this torture.

The morning light filled the room. I could almost see our star's rise in the horizon. The orange light it sent out glowed through the pores of the window. Another Tide to mull over how I wished I had treated my wife differently — with love and kindness. Another Tide to rue my many failures.

The painted vista slipped away. The pale of blue took up its position as sky color. I could not remember when I had taken the time to notice such things. Before the war? On Westla? Before Shaara was stolen from me? Yes. I remembered.

In the little cottage, the wolf's cottage, we had sat and watched sky colors. Shaarac had been only a baby then, suckling on my beautiful wife's breast. (Beautiful, the non-Shapechanger word. Had I used it then? I did not remember.) But we had sat together, enjoying the forest of trees, the sunrise, and the way it felt to love each other.

In the Palace of my brother, the heat was filling the room, letting me know that time was marching forward. Afternoon. I remembered the Tide I had taken Shaara to the Carnival. She tried her first alcohol and did not like it. She yearned for a piece of jewelry. I turned down her request. Shapechanger do not accumulate, I said, ignoring the yearning in her eyes.

Tren had not ignored the look in her eyes. He knew what would bring her joy. He gifted it to her. I thought he was crazy, selling the casino so he could buy her a landoor. "She will never live here," I told him. "She lives on Westla."

But he did it anyway, fenced in a chunk of the field, and paid extravagantly to ship the beast here. "She may never see it," I warned him.

He shrugged. "Crimson will wait for her. When she comes, her eyes will light up at the sight of him. That will make it all worthwhile," Tren had said.

And I had mocked him.

Tren and I were of a similar age. He had known Shaara so much less time than I, yet he *saw* her when I did not.

# Teea

Shaara was the first to wonder where Shaarvan had gone. I told her not to worry that he was often busy doing government work or checking on the battlefront. The fort of earlier times in the war was no longer manned as it had once been. Confrontations popped up unexpectedly and unpredictably everywhere now, more than in the battleground where we'd fought so many skirmishes.

But as the hours passed and Shaarvan still had not returned to make contact with his sons, I became concerned. When he hadn't returned for dinner, I talked to Starnkor about it. My Second sent out tendrils to find Shaarvan's location. Then Pathe showed up with his new wife, Patha.

Introductions were made, and we sat about the table chatting about various things. Shaara asked if Pathe knew where Shaarvan was. My son told us of Shaarvan's earlier visit. We were discussing that when a soldier arrived at the door with information. Shaarvan's pilotcar was surrounded by dead bodies, and Shaarvan was missing.

"No!" Shaara cried out. I thought she might faint. She swayed, but Spelon was at her side at once. Thedar and Tren, the next closest, surrounded her. I don't think she felt their presence. She had gone inward, searching, seeking the tendrils of that connection that had anchored Shaarvan and her together so long during the war.

Starnkor returned with similar news, but he had found out more. The Commoners had taken Shaarvan to Thenos' palace.

The buzz of conversation was an angry welling, a cry, a saga of despair. The males' faces grew hard and stiffened not to show us their worry.

Spelon suggested that Shaara lie down and rest a bit. But when she looked up at him, her teary eyes were fierce with anger. She was not the girl I had so long ago known. Shaara was a newly made warrior. If a Commoner had come inside at the moment, she would have lashed him with her Power, I think. She was a Saberey.

A drone dropped a parcel. Soldiers brought it to us. Inside were the words: *We will trade Shaarvan of Altar for Queen Thenosa. No harm will come to her. She will be treated royally.*

# *Chapter Fourteen*

## Shaara

It was like a beacon in the night. The moment I heard the contents of that note, I remembered my dream. I think I had dreamed it way back on Westla. But it had suddenly returned into my mind, vividly real. I knew what would happen. Like a memory of something I'd done, I saw the steps clearly in my mind. My bondmates would try to rescue Shaarvan, forbidding me to go anywhere near Thenos' Palace.

Spelon would be incensed when I argued, reverting to his former command/obey sequence. He would lock me in the room, then go off with Thedar, Tren, Pathe, and Starnkor. The others and I would remain at the house in the dark about what was going on. But Tura would break me out. The Priestess Tura was the key.

Her face had always been blurred in my dreams. I hadn't been able to see her, but I had known there was someone there, someone I hadn't met yet. I knew her now. Priestess Tura was the missing component. She would be the one to help me save Shaarvan.

While the males set out to break down the palace gate to wage war against the Commoners with an all-out final battle, Starnkor and Spelon would die, and Shaarvan would come out crippled, but we weak females were supposed to twiddle our thumbs and wait.

That wasn't an acceptable outcome. I had a choice, and I would take it.

Dinner over, everything played out just as I'd dreamed. The progression was like dominoes, plunging in a slow-motion fall.

When Tura came to unlock me from my room, she read into my mind, nodded her head, and said, "I dreamed it, too. I will cover for you, Shaara. Go do what you need to do."

I dressed in a pair of Spelon's slacks, cutting off the overly long legs and belting the pants so they wouldn't fall off. They were still like wearing a bathtub. I felt bulky and awkward, but such things were unimportant when there were lives to save.

Slipping out of the house seemed easier than it should have been, but then Tura was on my side. She was entertaining the others with tales from her time with Tessa. Tura and Tessa had been good friends for many Passes. I wished I could hear those stories. I wanted to see Tessa young and adventurous. Maybe another time?

When I entered the field where Crimson was, he galloped right up to me. I grabbed a bridle this time, needing to direct him. I took a saddle, too, but found that I could no longer lift it up onto his back. I could have asked Crimson to kneel and attach it with several ups and downs, but I didn't have time for that. I slipped on the bridle, left the saddle in the dust, and mounted.

I had no idea where the gate to the field was. I hadn't seen it on my ride before. But the fence was not that high. It was jumpable, and Crimson was willing. He seemed excited about breaking free from his confinement. He had always been an incredible jumper.

We walked a bit after that, wanting to avoid the noise of his hooves on the hardened path. Then, far enough away not to make much difference, we followed the path to the end of its length. There, we found the public train. It was running irregularly now, I'd been told, so I would stay at a distance from the tracks, but shadowing it would take us in the right direction to Thenos' Palace.

I had never been there, but it used to be the government center across from the Shapechanger Hall of Records. Shaarvan had taken me there Passes ago when Shaarac was still a baby. I probably would not have remembered it sufficiently well to find my way, but the dream had given me a map that was far easier to follow than a far-off memory.

A landoor is not as fast as a train, but Crimson's hooves swallowed the distance. Unfortunately, the pilot car the bondmates would take would be much faster, but they were planning to collect two battalions to go with them. Would I get to the Palace before them? I could not push Crimson any faster. It would not be safe for either of us. But we were almost there. Around the bend . . .

Commoners stood watching me gallop up. No pipe weapons were raised. No cries of alarm. They were waiting for me, sure that I would come.

I dismounted ordered one of the men to walk Crimson. The man paled. His eyes grew round with fear. Thankfully, another volunteered, stepping up to allow me to hand over the landoor's reins. I patted Crimson, kissed his nose, then hugged him again.

"Be good, Crimson. I will return," I said, although I had no idea if that would be true. The dream had gotten me this far, but it had not shown beyond. I had surged ahead of the crossroads. The males would not die. There would no battle. But what came after that, I could not say.

Three males opened the heavy gates for me. They bowed, although they looked rather askance at my clothing. On top of that, I probably stank of landoor. It's not a good portrayal of a Queen.

I saw Shaarvan almost at once. They had chains on him. His wrists were fastened tightly. He was bound to a throne.

"Shaara," Shaarvan said, shaking his head.

"Release him," I ordered in my most Queenly voice.

Two people rushed forward, undid the chains, and then unfastened the rope on his wrists. Shaarvan stood up stiffly and ungainly for him. "Where are your guardians? Why are you here alone?" he asked.

"Do not dare to address the Queen in this manner," one of the Commoners said. I looked back and saw that many of the males had followed me inside.

"He is my legal husband. I will allow him to say whatever he wishes and however he wishes to say it," I said, glaring at the one who had spoken.

"Yes, my Queen," the man said, bowing so low I thought he would topple over.

Shaarvan was once more shaking his head at me. "Endless adaptations. You are a marvel, my wife."

He sounded almost like before, back in the Tides, when he spoke with me across endless space. Had he forgiven me? Was it possible?

I took a step closer, watching his eyes. I wished we had privacy. I wished I felt more sure what he would do if I kissed his lips, but *Courage was pursuing that which you feared,* Thal had once told me. I was certain it applied here.

Another step forward. Shaarvan's eyes were soft gray, alert, but not rejecting. Did I have a chance to touch my lips to his before he turned and walked away?

"I will not reject you, Shaara. I cannot anymore. Besides, it is your turn to refuse me. I have treated you vilely. I have not been the husband you deserve. Yet, you have loved me and endured my cruelty throughout all the time that we shared. I ask your forgiveness. I am humbled before your kindnesses and the love you shower on everyone. I thank you for killing , , , " he stopped. "That might not be politic to speak of right now."

He flashed a weak smile, an unsure one, then continued. "You are a Priestess. You can go and do whatever you like now. I have no control and can no longer expect your obedience, yet I will husband you if you wish. Or you may discard me as I deserve."

While he'd been speaking, I continued my steps forward. When he reached the end of his words, my lips met his. I breathed in his scent, and then I plunged my tongue into his mouth. I was overly assertive for a female. I knew that, yet . . .

He didn't seem to mind. His arms encircled me. He pulled me closer. He robbed me of breath — in a good way.

We forgot about our audience, tuned out voices, demands, queries, and the shuffling of restless bodies.

A sudden shout, a bellow, males in half-change . . . "How did you get here first?" Tenor demanded.

Only that broke Shaarvan and me apart, but Shaarvan's arm slid across my waist in the old Shapechanger hold. It felt familiar, almost comfortable. I leaned my head against his shoulder. It was too early to say, but I think I heard his heart beating, "Shaara, Shaara, Shaara."

Shaarvan looked down at me and smiled. "It never stopped telling me that, my wife. It has always been steadfast."

He touched his lips to my forehead, then said. "You never answered me. Am I to be discarded, or do you forgive my many, many mistakes — my cruelty and thoughtlessness, my failure to protect you from kidnapping, and . . .?"

I stopped him with a finger over his mouth. "Yes," I said simply.

# *Chapter Fifteen*

## Tren

The Commoners were at first shaken by the Queen's obvious infatuation with their enemy, the Great General Shaarvan. They wanted to dissuade her, but all their efforts were in vain. She had endless power. What could they say in the end?

Then, they demanded that Shaara take up residency in the palace. She was not against that directly, she told them, but then added that she would never again be separated from her landoor, and since the Palace was in the city, there was no place to quarter him or ride.

Again, that disquieted them. Thenos had not mentioned Shaara's fascination with a landoor. The Commoners were quarreling, shooting out solutions, but none of them could find a way to allow the landoor to stay at the Palace. When she told them that she absolutely would not stay without her beloved landoor, they acquiesced. What else could they do? It was obvious that they would do anything to keep her happy.

I imagine that a fancy stable and arena would be first on their list of building projects, right after a certain cottage in the forest that they promised to rebuild for her. That was Shaara's first demand.

Perhaps that small cabin, a piece of nostalgia for Shaara, could be a place to visit, to roam the forest and to be with the Saberey, but she would never be allowed to live there. As she said, she must be with her landoor.

My soul filled with happiness that my gift of Crimson Black was so well-appreciated, but the biggest thrill came from her reunion with Shaarvan. A radiant light shone from inside her. We all saw it. There was no question that the two were meant for each other. Even the Commoners accepted that it must be so.

But they remained unshakeable that she must become their Queen. They bent to the landoor, to the small cabin, to Shaarvan at her side, but they held steadfast in their belief that Altar's way forward was with Queen Thenosa.

Such details would slowly come together. I had no doubts. Shaara had that way about her. Already, the Commoners, who in all this time had never met her, had fallen under her spell. Ah, the stories and myths we would soon be hearing of the way she had come galloping up to the royal gates astride a great black beast. The landoor would probably be breathing fire and rearing to the sky while the diminutive Queen curbed his flashing hooves and tamed his raging spirit with her soft, gentle voice.

But Shaara has always been more than a smile and a kind-hearted, stubborn recklessness. She was a plotter and planner with a keen mind. Already, she had gone for the jugular, determined that if she must be bound to the Commoners' wishes, she would at least drive Altar from out of the Dark Ages, as she put it. I suspected she would first establish rights of females and woe to the Commoners who tried to deny her.

"Who is the head of the Commoners?" she wanted to know right off.

The mob of males crowding the main hall cast glances at each other, none wishing to volunteer for possible death. Throats cleared, but no one spoke. Some stepped away, retreating back to the door, only to be stopped by the soldiers the bondmates had brought to rescue Shaarvan.

Shaara walked over to the large throne. Shaarvan, at her request, took his place beside her in the smaller one. They smiled at each other, then waited. Shaarvan was dusty and dirty from his take-down next to the pilot car. Perhaps his captors had rolled him about in the dust. One side of his face was red and puffy. His shirt was torn, and his pants ripped. He looked like one of the street urchins of Freinanan.

Beside him on the bigger throne sat the waif I used to know on Freinana. Her clothes looked like rags from the resale bin. I knew they were Spelon's cast-offs that she had cut (badly and unevenly.) Her face was streaked with dirt. She had grass or horse saliva stains on her shirt. I was sure she stunk of landoor.

It was an odd juxtaposition, these two ragamuffins on the elite thrones of Thenos. Sparkling jewels atop the two stately stone thrones jutted up in the back, curving above them with arches that shielded the two regally. The Royal insignia on top made a statement that whoever sat in its seats commanded all.

But the Commoners seemed only content that their Queen was finally present. I doubt they had any idea what was in store for them. It made me smile to think about it.

The wait for a response to Shaara's question about the head of the Commoners had been overly long, but neither Shaara nor Shaarvan uttered a word. At last a single man was pushed forward by three burly Commoners. "This is Pelo. He is the Head of the Commoners," the three said.

"I did not arrange for the kidnapping of your husband," the man cried out, weeping in his fear. His face showed markings of how hard he had fought not to be dragged forward. His cheeks were red and scratched. One eye puffed out, having obviously been punched. Pelo

212

may have plotted for Shaara to be placed on that throne, but yet, at the sight of her there, he was struck with fear so great he cowered and whimpered before her.

"Good. What is your full name?" Shaara asked.

"Stephanos Pelo," he responded with a bow that touched his head to floor.

"Okay, first rule from your Queen," Shaara said. "There will be no more deep bowing. I am a person. You are a person. A brief nod of respect can be your greeting."

Shaarvan, beside her, cleared his throat. Shaara turned her head, her eyes all soft and gooey with love, as she gazed at him.

"Perhaps, as we do in the battalions, the fist clap might be used to assign authority?" he said, demonstrating the gesture they used.

I doubt Shaara cared about such signs of authority, but she did not want to negate anything Shaarvan wanted, so she said almost automatically. "Yes, we will make that the royal greeting, but no head touching the floor ever again."

"What is it that the Commoners want? Why did you demand me to come? What do you want from me?" Shaara demanded of Pelo.

As usual, Shaara's questions came in a rush. It left the man before her, sputtering as he tried to figure out which question to answer first.

Shaarvan reached out and took Shaara's hand. That silenced her. She glanced at him, smiled, and, I think, forgot that a man still stood before her, entrapped by her questions and by her having demanded his presence before her.

Moments passed while Shaara and Shaarvan stared into each other's eyes, lost in their enchantment for each other. Did Stephanos

Pelo see that? Did he realize she was like a new bride, frozen in that chrysalis of reawakened love?

Probably, he was not even aware of the Queen's thoughts at that moment. He was sweating rivers of water, his brow a faucet of drip. If Shaara had seen that, she would have moved to release him from his terror, but she had forgotten him, forgotten that she was even in the Palace of Thenos.

She was too newly entwined with the love of her life, too eager to crawl into his lap and feel his arms around her. And Shaarvan, I could see, was no better. He had suppressed his feelings too long to be the stoic Shapechanger who rose above such emotions.

"We . . . we . . . need you to be our Queen," the man finally got out.

His words broke the chain that held the two throned ones enthralled. Shaara blinked and looked away from Shaarvan. Her eyes once again discovered the Commoner before her. She tilted her head as she stared at him.

"I am here. I sit on your throne. Now, what do you want?"

"We . . . we . . . want. . ."

"Fairness," said someone from the crowd.

"Equality," said another.

Shaara nodded. "Bring those two up here," she called out, demanding the guards with a firmness I'd never seen from her before. I wondered if it was her Priestess training that had stiffened her spine and commandeered her gentleness, for there was none of that at the minute. She suddenly felt almost like a stranger to me. Had a half hour on the throne changed her whole personality?

The audacious speakers were not so daring once they were found. The soldiers half-carted them forward. One of them bowed low, his head touching the ground.

"No," Shaara shouted. "I told you . . ."

"Shaara," Shaarvan said. Nothing more, but it was enough. She inhaled heavily, dropped her eyes, and stared down at her hands for a moment.

"Rise," she said when she looked up because her temper had caused not only the two new Commoners to collapse to the floor but also the entire front rows of the amassed Commoners.

I suppose they were all remembering Thenos at that moment. He had been harsh in his treatment of the Commoners who adored him, often slashing them with various torments and even stabbing them with his claws when his anger rode him. They had feared him yet worshipped him. It was unquestionably strange.

Shaara was not like that. I wanted to tell them, but I remained silent, wondering what I could do to stop this fiasco. Shaara needed time to recover, time to be alone with Shaarvan and to sleep. I could see the fatigue written across her face. Her eyes sagged with the desire to close her eyes and lay her head down. She was barely able to hold herself up in the chair with any correspondence to her new position. It was obvious to me that her adrenaline had crashed, and only willpower held her now in place. My poor little waif.

Once again, she was my girl, the one who needed a chest to cry on, my strength to lean on. Shaarvan would be that in the future, but his energy was flagging. I could see that his captivity had not been kind to him, and no doubt, the breakdown of his old restraints had defeated him almost as greatly. He'd probably been tortured and mistreated, been dragged through a nightmare of not knowing which moment would be his last.

215

Death had acquitted him, but he was as new to this role as Shaara. Both of them were already forging new identities. Perhaps it would be even harder for him. Shaara had already been striving to change her life. Shaarvan, whether he realized it or not, had been retreating, hiding from it.

The crowd in the chamber had doubled. A few females stepped forward and offered homage using the sign Shaarvan had suggested. Ignoring the three men, all more or less collapsed at the foot of the thrones, these females asked if Queen Thenosa would kindly set a date for her investiture. Shaara glanced again at her husband, hesitating to answer. "I will consider," she said after Shaarvan explained what the word meant.

I wanted Shaarvan to speak or Shaara to tell the crowd that they needed to rest. But I doubt they had the energy any longer to end the session. They might slowly wilt down in their giant thrones and fall into sleep. I suppose the crowd would all wait, watching their new Queen, waiting for the spectacle to continue. But that could not happen. The two needed to go home to recuperate and regenerate the energy that this night had stolen from them.

There was no one else who would dare suggest it. I stepped forward, pushing my way through the assembled masses, elbowing when needed, until I stood directly in front of Shaara. I made the new gesture, although I was tempted to bow down and touch my head to the floor, just to see her explode.

She smiled at me halfheartedly, the candle of her vitality flickering. "Tren," she said, sighing with exhaustion.

"As your brother, I must announce to these good people that it is time you were home in bed. They must see that you are fatigued. Perhaps another date can be set for your return to the Palace."

"I want that very much, my brother," she said. Thank you. Please speak with these men and take down their names. I want to talk to them, but you're right. I can't do any more now. I am . . . too tired."

She looked out at the crowd. The room was filled beyond capacity. She saw their need, their desire to reach out to her. She brushed a hint of Priestess Power across them, gentling them, assuring them, and soothing their angst.

"I promise to return in a twoTide," Shaara said. "Leave now that I might go rest for my return to you."

It was as easy as that. The assembled masses turned and exited the chamber as if they were robotic transports carrying loads at Space Port. No pushing, no elbowing, only smooth progress toward the huge gates of the Palace and then dwindling numbers until they simply dissipated into the city. Only the three men at the front remained. I went to them to perform my new duty.

But still, I watched, ready to go to Shaara if she needed me.

"My love," Shaara said, her voice tiny and fragile with weariness. "I have to ride Crimson home. There is no other way to get him there. Will you meet me at home?"

Shaarvan's visage suddenly transformed into storm clouds. He was once more the great Shapechanger Lord glaring down at a disobedient wife. I prepared to launch myself.

But Shaarvan suddenly halted, blinked, and rethought. "This is going to take me some adjustment time," he more or less apologized, although he hadn't actually said a word after her announcement.

She rose, came towards him, and kissed his lips. "I know," she said. "We shall adapt to this new world together, but I am yours no matter how long that adjustment takes us."

They parted with a tender kiss, then Shaara suddenly almost herself again ran to the gate and shouted for Crimson Black.

She rode the landoor home with us in a pilot car, well back so as not to frighten the beast. Our lights displayed her route, although she'd told me once that a landoor always knew his way back to the stable.

I noticed that Crimson was careful with her. There was no prancing in his gait. Perhaps he was as tired as she was. Novelty was wearing on us all. Yet, I think the beast was poky and calm as a rental nag because he knew Shaara was almost ill with exhaustion.

As I'd said earlier; The animal showed signs of sentience. He possibly felt his rider's low energy level. For whatever reason, this landoor was far different than the one we'd seen out in the field. Even Shaarvan was relieved to see the great care the animal took with his wife.

When we arrived home, the hour was late. I relieved everyone's stress, explaining that all had gone well. Tura, seeing Shaara's condition, handed her some juice and a cookie and ordered her to meet her need. Teea rushed to Shaarvan and saw that he ate something, too. Once more, the chairs at the table were filled with anxious Shapechanger. But no one pestered them for details.

After Shaara finished the drink she went to Spelon. He stood as she approached, shooting a questioning glance at Shaarvan before giving his full attention to Shaara. She first touched her lips to his, then drew back. "I cannot be with you anymore," she told him. "I'm sorry."

Spelon picked up her hand and kissed it. "I understand. It was Shaarvan from the moment I met you. Never once did you waver. We Shapechanger respect faithfulness. You are loved, my Shaara."

Shaarvan had stood when his wife did, but he made no move toward her as she spoke with Spelon. He waited, perhaps unsure in that moment.

"I respect that your husband has rejoined you, as is right," Spelon said. "I withdraw my claim on you, but I ask that you allow me to remain in the family. I could not live away from you now, Shaara. I could not live."

It was a sweet moment, handled well by both of them and throughout it, Shaarvan made no move to object to Shaara's closeness to Spelon or to the words that were said. His fists clamped, a faint residue of Saberey dusted his face, but he accepted all that his wife did without a growl or a chastisement.

"Nothing will change now that Shaarvan and I are back together. My dear bondmates, you are all beloved to me and the children. That must continue always. We are Trendacons as Tem and the Saberey said. We shall remain family always."

Shaarvan seconded her words. I think he was too tired to do so formally, but we saw that he harbored no ill feelings for Spelon's tending of his wife. His eyes toured the group, and he said, "We are all Trendacons. All family."

I noticed as we withdrew to our separate rooms that Shaarvan did not presume to be invited into Shaara's bedroom that night. I believe the two remained separate, but by the next morning, by the time day had rosied its cheeks, the two were as if they had never parted. I suspected that Shaarvan had at some time snuck into her room and convinced Shaara to enjoy their rebonding.

Shaara was true to her promise to the Commoners. She returned to the Palace in a twoTide and began the laborious work needed to soothe the ache of war. She talked with the three Commoners who had been brought forward and added more, including a female, to the list of those to be in the new Assembly. Progress was being made. It was a beginning, but with Shaara, I had expectations that it would continue.

So, sometimes, a history ends in smooth trajectories. Sometimes not. A sevenTide later, Shaara decided that since Tura and Pathe could not cause Tevor to awaken, she must do so. It was a great strain on her to attempt to pass that belief into reality, and she tried many times.

Tura and she both put their minds to the process. With Teea funneling her Power as well, they bent over from the strain of it, but they could not bring Tevor out of his coma. With tears and resignation, Teea disconnected her husband's feeding tube. After that, his decline was swift. An hour later, he slipped away, never once having awakened to look into the eyes of his loving wife.

Perhaps that was best. I was told that Tevor had hated her tears. He would not have been pleased to see them.

On Altar, burial is still the path for the dead. Tevor joined Crimson in finding himself in a broad expanse of meadow. He was placed near the gate, the one Shaara did not know the placement of. His burial plot was close enough that Teea could walk to it and grieve as she chose.

Starnkor was no longer her Second then. He had become Teea's full Husband. He had always treated her well and seemed to be a wise soul. Shaara had already given him a position in the government. In fact, all of us were Elders of the Board with Shaara at its Head as Queen.

The saga of the Trendacons was temporarily quiet. Shaara remained undecided about returning to Westla, but Shaarvan thought she would one day. Mandar still waited for her. And Tem and Tessa still wrote.

But Shaarac and Shaandar were quite a handful, and Shaara was already pregnant with a new baby. This meant that riding time on Crimson had temporarily stopped, but she came out to brush him every Tide.

# *Chapter Sixteen*

### Tren (continued)

After the Thenos Palace event (the Palace name which the Commoners refused to change,) Spelon and I were crushed. We had both lost Shaara in a way, although we knew that neither one of us had actually ever owned her, nor could. But we had done what grieving Shapechanger always did. We formed a friendship over drink.

We first filled our steins and agreed that the important thing was that Shaara was happy. Then, we pledged to remain by her side no matter what was to come. And then, I forget what we vowed, probably something to do with the boys. But after numerous mugs, a lot of singing, a few tears from the dust in our eyes, and a new bond of friendship cemented between us, we passed through most of our grief.

We would also remain in her life. Wherever she was, we would be. That was another vow Spelon and I made. I am not sure, but I think that Tenor and Thedar were with us at that point. They told us they were celebrating Shaara and Shaarvan's reunion rather than grieving for any loss of Shaara. But I guess it was the same thing. We bonded, we four, in Team Shaara. Or should I say Queen Thenosa? It was all the same.

# Shaara

Life was good. Shaarvan and I were still adjusting to our changing roles. I urged Shaarvan to assist as much as possible. I wished he could take over this ruling business. I was so unsuited for it.

The whole thing still made no sense to me that I was supposed to rule a planet I'd spent less than a Pass on when I was nineteen Terran years old and already pregnant with a new baby. I hardly knew the language at that point. I hadn't known the customs, and had still been trying to process becoming a Shapechanger.

The Commoners yielded officially to my marriage to Shaarvan, accepted my need to reside with my landoor, and although there are some who refused to call me anything but Queen Thenosa, most allowed me to call myself Shaara of Shaarvan. It was more difficult when Shaarvan tried to change Thaandar's name legally to Shaandar. On that, the Commoners would not relent. So, Thaandar took on another name. At home, he was Shaandar, and in public, he was Prince Thenon.

The fact that I was never Thenos' wife and Shaandar was not conceived by Thenos through some mystical space nighttime meetings was no longer even volleyed back and forth. It seemed that when a falsehood was said enough times, it became the Truth.

One day, I went out to the backyard to brush Crimson Black, as I did most Tides. Spelon, Tenor, Tren, and Thedar were all standing at the fence with big grins on their normally expressionless faces.

That set off all my alarm bells until I saw that Crimson Black was just fine. But standing next to him was Mandar, my landoor from

Westla. I shrieked with joy, which brought out Teea and Starnkor. Shaarvan followed, as did Shaarac and the maid who was carrying Shaandar.

A whole circus of shrieks of joy erupted from my vocal chords before I could silence my excitement. When Mandar and Crimson Black finally calmed down after my screaming joy fest and stopped blowing through flaring nostrils and showing off with hindleg kicks in the air, plus several rears and a couple of head tosses, I quieted them with a couple of hand pats, hugs, kisses, and some Altarian carrots, (blue ones, but the landoors didn't mind).

With calls to be careful shooting at me from all the spectators. Spelon ordered me not to mount either landoor like I could with a belly upset most days with Shaarvor, Shaarvan's name for the baby inside me. Shaarvan said nothing, but I could feel his concern. But neither Mandar nor Crimson Black would ever harm me. They were both special.

The bondmates had also sent for the fat old landoor we called Chair because he didn't do much more than act like a chair. He was to be Shaarac's mount. I hoped my son would someday have more enthusiasm for riding than he showed at the moment.

Luckily the three landoors all got along splendidly, and Crimson Black and Mandar became best buddies.

But that is a tale for another time. It includes how a girl from Southern California could end up on a faraway planet with four strong bodyguards who loved her, a husband who adored his wife, two, almost three, fine sons — and friends, relatives, and acquaintances from all over Altar and the artificial planet, Westla.

Sometimes beginnings are really, really tough, but if you're lucky and the fates smile down at you, the middles can be remarkably and perfectly spectacular.

To read more about what's going to happen next:

# Priestess Tura

## *Book 8*

### *of the Shaarvan Series*